“In her riveting debut, Bronsky giv[illegible]
17-year-old Russian immigrant livin[illegible]
rates a brutal story with a sharp, ca[illegible] . . . Sascha’s
hunger for life shines through her relentless fight to leave behind a painful childhood—a struggle complicated by an unexpected twist in the final act—making for a stark, moving tale of resiliency and survival.”
—*Publishers Weekly* (Starred Review)

“What a huge talent! This reader held his breath from start to finish. Bronsky is blessed with a language that is urgent and exuberant; she never sinks into banality or presumptuousness . . . *Broken Glass Park* is the most astonishing debut in years.”
—*Nürnberger Nachrichten*

“*Broken Glass Park* is candid and insolent, provocative and acute.”—*Echo Online* (Germany)

“*Broken Glass Park* tells the story of a variegated humanity living in and around a ghetto-estate in Germany. What makes the book even more interesting is the author’s background. Born in 1978, raised in the Russian industrial town of Sverdlovsk (today Yekaterinburg) at the foot of the Ural Mountains, Bronsky moved to Germany with her family when she was thirteen years old. So, do we have a young literary lion telling the hard-hitting story of her own rough childhood on the dangerous fringes of German society? Whatever the answer, not a few jurors at the notorious Ingeborg-Bachmann-Award competition, held each year in Klagenfurt, wanted her as their chosen candidate . . . The jury praised her novel, calling it ‘refreshing,’ ‘brilliant’ and ‘gratifying.’”—*Der Spiegel*

“A tough book, but also a touching story of a 17-year-old forced to grow up much too fast.”—*Focus* (Germany)

"I once lived in Germany, and this book gives voice to an immigrant experience so startlingly vivid that my memory of the country is deepened retroactively. Wonderful voice, wonderful characters, wonderful book."
—Sarah McNally, McNally Jackson Books (New York)

"*Broken Glass Park* has filled vast numbers of booksellers with enthusiasm—weeks before the novel's publication, Bronsky was tipped as the 'most exciting newcomer of the season . . .' There's a double murder, blood, a suicide, a young woman flips out and smashes reams of windows. Anything else? Yes, an amazingly dauntless heroine: Sascha, seventeen, of Russian descent, resident in a German ghetto. If *Broken Glass Park* were a song, it would be fast, brilliantly composed, rebellious and in parts ear-splittingly loud."
—*Brigitte Magazine* (Germany)

"I loved this deeply moving story that is sad in its details yet exhilarating in its expression and resolution . . . What a tough, brilliant heroine! She turns anger and resilience into an art form. This is a rich and expressive story that is ultimately triumphant in utterly unique ways. From first page to last this story had me."—Sheryl Cotleur, Book Passage (Corte Madera)

"A remarkable debut. *Broken Glass Park* beautifully captures the volatile mix of innocence and experience that's the privilege and the burden of youth. Sascha Naimann truly is a heroine for our time: tough and vulnerable in equal measure, she refuses to give up on her dreams, even though she's living through a nightmare. Her story, told with wit and flair, will grab you as it grabbed me."
—Alicia Erian, author of the *New York Times* notable book *Towelhead*

# BROKEN GLASS PARK

Alina Bronsky

# BROKEN GLASS PARK

*Translated from the German*
*by Tim Mohr*

Europa Editions
116 East 16th Street
New York, N.Y. 10003
www.europaeditions.com
info@europaeditions.com


First Publication 2010 by Europa Editions

Translation by Tim Mohr
Original title: *Scherbenpark*


Library of Congress Cataloging in Publication Data is available
ISBN 978-1-933372-96-9

Bronsky, Alina
Broken Glass Park

The translation of this work was supported by a grant from the Goethe-Institut which is funded by the German Ministry of Foreign Affairs

Book design by Emanuele Ragnisco
www.mekkanografici.com

Prepress by Plan.ed – Rome

Printed in Canada

# BROKEN GLASS PARK

For Galina, Leonid, and Michael.
In memory of Nadezhda Zotova.

Sometimes I think I'm the only one in our neighborhood with any worthwhile dreams. I have two, and there's no reason to be ashamed of either one. I want to kill Vadim. And I want to write a book about my mother. I already have a title: The Story of an Idiotic Redheaded Woman Who Would Still Be Alive If Only She Had Listened to Her Smart Oldest Daughter. Or maybe that's more of a subtitle. But I have plenty of time to figure it out because I haven't started writing yet.

Most of the people who live around here don't have any dreams at all. I've asked. And the dreams of the ones who do have them are so pathetic that if I were in their shoes I'd rather not have any.

Anna's dream, for instance, is to marry rich. Her dream man would be a judge in his mid-thirties, and, fingers crossed, not too terribly ugly.

Anna is seventeen, same as I am, and she says she'd get married immediately if a guy like that came along. That way she could finally move out of the Emerald and into the judge's penthouse apartment. Nobody but me knows that Anna sometimes takes the tram downtown and wanders a dozen times around the courthouse in the hope that her judge will finally come out and discover her, give her a red rose, take her out for ice cream, and then invite her back to his penthouse.

She says you'll never get lucky if you don't fight for it; if you don't fight, the moment will just pass you by.

"Do you have any idea what Emerald means, you stupid

cow?" I ask her. "It's the most elegant way to cut a diamond, and a fine gemstone itself. That's got to be appealing to you. You'll never live in another Emerald if you move out of this place."

"You just made that up. They would never in a million years have named this heap of concrete after a diamond cut," says Anna. "And by the way, when you know too much, you get old and wrinkled faster." That's a Russian saying.

As Anna's judge could take a while, for now she's sleeping with Valentin, who has a third-rate dream of his own. He wants a brand-new, snow-white Mercedes. First he'll have to get his driver's license. Which costs a lot. That's why he delivers advertising brochures door to door before school. Since the money to be made at that is barely a trickle, Valentin also cleans the house of an old married couple twice a week. The couple lives on the other side of town. He got the job through his mother, who cleans the place next door. Nobody can know he's a housecleaner—if the guys at school found out, they'd never let him live it down, and Anna would split up with him.

Valentin usually has a look on his face as if someone just shoved a cactus down his pants. I think it's because he realizes that even if he eventually gets enough money together to take driver's ed classes and get his license, it would take another two lifetimes of cleaning houses to buy a white Mercedes. And then maybe in his third lifetime he'd be able to hop in and actually take a spin.

Peter the Great, on the other hand, dreams of a natural blonde with dark eyes. He was with Anna before. She has brown eyes but she's not natural—not natural blond, anyway. Now he's with another girl, one from his class at school. But it's less convenient, as she lives downtown rather than here in the Emerald. Since they got together, he complains he spends half his life on the tram. But while he's on it, he keeps his eyes peeled for other blondes.

He was never interested in me—my hair's too dark.

My name is Sascha Naimann. I'm not a guy, even though everyone in this country seems to think so when they hear my name. I've given up counting how often I've had to explain it to people. Sascha is a short form of Alexander *and* Alexandra. I'm an Alexandra. But my name is Sascha—that's what my mother always called me, and that's what I want to be called. When people address me as Alexandra, I don't even react. That used to happen a lot more when I was new in school. These days it only happens when there's a new teacher.

Sometimes I think I don't ever want to meet any new people because I'm sick of having to explain everything from scratch. Why my name is Sascha and how long I've lived in Germany and how come I speak German so well—ten times better than all the other Russian Germans put together.

I know German because my head is filled with a gray matter shaped like a big walnut. Macroscopically it has lots of ridges and microscopically loads of synapses. I probably have a few million more than Anna—definitely. Besides German, I also know physics, chemistry, English, French, and Latin. If I ever get a B on an assignment, the teacher comes over to me and apologizes.

I'm particularly good at math. When we came to Germany seven years ago, math was the only subject I could handle right away, in the fifth grade. Truth be told, I could have solved the eighth grade assignments. Back in Russia I was in a special math school.

In Germany I couldn't speak a word at first, but the numbers were the same. I always solved the equations first, and always correctly. I was the only one in class who had any idea what algebra and geometry were. My classmates acted as if they were diseases.

My mother laughed about it and said she found me a little scary. I was always scary in her eyes, though, because I thought much more logically than she did. She wasn't stupid, but she was too sentimental. She read at least one thick novel per week, played piano and guitar, knew a million songs, and was good at languages. Learned German real fast, for instance—and before that was able to communicate with people in passable English.

Math, physics, chemistry—she was no good at them. Just as she was no good at recognizing when it was time to show a man the door. These are all abilities I must have gotten from my father. All I know about him is that he had multiple doctorates and an unpleasant personality. "You got that, too," my mother used to say. "And the degrees will no doubt come at some point."

I'm the only one from our community who goes to the Alfred Delp school. It's a private Catholic school, and to this day I have no idea why they accepted me back then—pretty much illiterate, never baptized, looking completely out of step in a pink wool sweater my grandmother had knitted. Being led by the hand by a mother only able to speak broken English—very loudly, with a ridiculous accent—and who wore her flaming red hair down. In her other hand was a liter of milk in a plastic bag from a discount grocery store.

Along with my mother, hundreds of German Catholic architects, doctors, and lawyers had applied for spots at the school for their kids. All people who practically had *GENEROUS DONOR* written across their foreheads in big letters.

You see, at the Alfred Delp school there's no tuition, but "donations are welcome." And Mrs. Weimars, the school secretary who peered over the top of her glasses to size up my mother, me, and the plastic bag, must have quickly come to a realistic assessment of my mother's liquidity (as those of us at such elite schools call it).

Actually, after I started attending the school, my mother did give twenty euros the first year and twenty-two the next—

which was all she could afford. She couldn't really afford those amounts, to be honest, but my mother was a fundamentally giving person. "There's nothing I hate more than a leech" was one of her favorite sentences. "It's a quality you hate only in yourself," I would always answer. "Try hating it in others—like Vadim, for instance."

In retrospect, I think they accepted me at the school to try to create a little diversity. A lot of doctors, lawyers, and architects got rejection notices for their kids. In the end there were five sections of fifth graders, each one crammed full, and in mine, 5C, I was the only one with an "immigrant background." In 5A was a kid with an American father, and in 5B another with a French mother. In all my years there I've never seen a single black kid or anyone who looked even vaguely Middle Eastern. So in my class I was the heavyweight when it came to diversity.

On the first day of school my classmates stared at me as if I had just climbed out of a UFO. They asked me questions I couldn't understand at first. Soon I could have answered them, but by then they all thought I was standoffish. It took a while for them to learn otherwise.

Considering most of them had never seen a foreigner up close before, they were all pretty nice to me. One of the first sentences I was able to understand was a compliment about my sweater. Probably out of pity. A little later, when I had learned to talk, count, and write papers and was the only one who put commas in the right places, everyone acted like they were happy for me. And maybe it was sincere.

My mother was always saying I should have friends from school over to our place. But she only said that because she was clueless. She was always inviting friends over. Twice I'd been over to the homes of girls from my class—Melanie and Carla—and I couldn't possibly imagine having them over.

I'm not sure what threw me more: the neatness of Melanie's

room, the scent of the polished furniture—the type of furniture I thought existed only in catalogues or Anna's fantasies—the fact that they sat around an oval dining room table for lunch instead of in the kitchen, or her horse-pattern sheets. I'd never seen such colorful sheets before. At home we had white or light-blue checked sheets, all of which were old and faded. How you could possibly fall asleep with your eyes flitting around looking at all those horses?

Melanie's mother, by the way, was originally from Hungary. That came as a complete surprise—for one thing because Melanie had never mentioned it, and for another because she looked more stereotypically German than any other girl in our entire school. She was exactly what foreigners picture when they think of a young German girl—particularly foreigners who form that image from afar, having never been to Germany.

She had freshly cropped, always-neat, chin-length blond hair, blue eyes, rosy cheeks, and a crisply ironed jean jacket. She smelled of soap and spoke in a chirpy voice using sentences of mostly monosyllabic words, words that popped out of her mouth like peas. If I hadn't have seen her in the flesh myself, I would never have believed someone like her actually existed.

Her mom, on the other hand, spoke with an accent—though I didn't notice it the first time I went over there. Back then my own accent screeched as distractingly as a rusty bicycle. During lunch she stared at me with pity when she thought I wasn't looking. She asked me questions about the town where I had grown up, the weather there, my old school, and my mother.

I told her that my mother had studied art history, that back home she had acted in a theater group that kept getting banned, that she wanted to find a little company here to join. Melanie's mother took a sip of water and segued into a different line of questioning: wasn't life in our housing project dangerous? I told her it was a lot cleaner and nicer than where I'd lived back there. I always referred to Russia that way—"back there."

Melanie nibbled on her cheese-filled puff pastry and corrected her mother whenever she made a grammatical error. She also told her mother that they'd done a poll in class about what people wanted for their birthdays and seven students had said they wanted new stereos.

"So what?" said her mother, looking at Melanie through narrowed eyes.

"Don't you understand what that means?" said Melanie, opening her blue eyes wide. "A *new* stereo. Meaning they already *have* one. And I still don't have one."

"But you do have one in your room," I said. I couldn't talk very well, but I talked a lot.

"That's just an old system my cousin was getting rid of," Melanie said. "It doesn't have any of the features a stereo has to have these days."

After lunch we went back into her spotless room. She turned on the stereo. I found a stack of old teen magazines and started reading them. Melanie spun herself around on her desk chair and chatted on the phone with another friend. Considering we didn't have anything to say to each other, we made good use of the time. That evening Melanie's mother drove me home. When we got there she looked around, unsettled, and insisted on taking me to the door to make sure I got home to my mother.

But my mother wasn't home. I had a key.

"You should come over again," said Melanie's mother, patting my cheek.

"Thanks," I said, thinking to myself, Not until there's a new stack of magazines.

After that I looked at our apartment in a different light.

I pictured spotless Melanie in her pressed jean jacket taking the elevator with me. I pictured the way she would look around, fidgeting, like her mother. The way the scent of her soap would fight with the smell of urine in the hallway—and lose. I pictured her coming through the door of our apartment, catching sight of the couch we'd found discarded by a dumpster and the little table in front of it that would collapse if you even looked at it too hard. Books on the floor. The little TV and stack of videocassettes—even back then nobody had VHS tapes anymore. The cabinet with no door. My stepfather's socks drying on the radiator. My brother's sweatpants draped over a chair. We had five chairs, each one different because we'd found them separately, each left out on the street the night before a heavy garbage pickup.

We always ate in the kitchen, except when we had guests over for a party—in which case we had to clear out the main room to be able to fit extra chairs borrowed from neighbors. Our kitchen table was usually covered with jars of jam, letters, postcards, half-empty bottles, and old newspapers. We had twenty plates; none matched any of the others. My mother had bought them all individually at the flea market.

We didn't have a dishwasher back then, and sometimes all twenty plates would stack up in the sink before my mother washed them up. Sometimes I did it, but not very often. And never when Vadim told me to—the same Vadim who left the frying pan crusted with the remains of his fried eggs. Though when his foul mouth started muttering my mother's name menacingly, I cleaned up real fast.

I hate men.

Anna says good men do exist. Nice, friendly men who cook and help clean up and who earn money. Men who want to have children and give gifts and plan vacations. Who wear clean clothes, don't drink, and even look halfway decent. Where on earth are they, I ask. She says they're out there—if not in our town then in Frankfurt. But she doesn't know any personally, unless you count people she's seen on TV.

That's why I always repeat the words my mother used to say: I don't need a man.

Of course, though she always said that, she never stuck to it.

Ever since I decided to kill Vadim, I've felt a lot better. I also promised Anton, my nine-year-old little brother, that I'd do it. And I think he feels better now, too. When I told him, he opened his eyes wide and asked, breathless, "How are you going to do it?"

I acted as if I had everything under control. "There's a thousand ways I could do it," I told him. "I could poison him, suffocate him, strangle him, stab him, push him off a balcony, run him over in a car."

"You don't have a car," said my brother Anton—and he was right.

"I can't get at him at the moment anyway," I said. "You know he's still in prison. He'll be there for years."

"Is that how long it's going to take?" said Anton.

"Yeah," I said, "but it's better that way—I'll have plenty of time to plan it out. It's not that easy to kill somebody when you've never done it before, you know."

"It'll be easier the second time around," said Anton like an expert.

"I just want to pull it off this one time," I said. "I don't want to make a hobby out of it."

I was relieved that Anton also thought it was a good idea. Vadim is his father, after all. But the little guy hates him just as much as I do. Maybe even more. He had already been a basket case beforehand, because unlike me he was always afraid of Vadim.

These days Anton's still in bad shape, showing no signs of improvement, and I sometimes ask myself whether all the therapy will do any good at all. He stutters, can't concentrate in school, wets his bed, and starts to shake whenever someone raises their voice. All this despite the fact that he claims not to remember anything. I always tell him: count yourself lucky if that's the case. I'm happy I can't remember anything, either—even though I was there.

I can discuss one of my dreams with Anton. But not the other one. Because anytime the word "mama" is mentioned in his vicinity, he freezes and just sits there dead still like a statue—as if he's just been kissed by the Snow Queen. My mother often read us the fairytale of the Snow Queen. She loved Hans Christian Andersen, loved that story in particular. Whenever somebody was mean, she would say they probably had a piece of the mirror in their eye or heart—she meant the mirror from the Snow Queen, the one the evil troll shattered. That's just how she was.

To shield him, I smack anyone who says the word "mama" in front of Anton. Not adults, obviously—I just shout at them. It always works. It's the least I can do for my little brother. Well, that and not chasing him out when he comes crying to my room at night, crawls into bed next to me, and then is so frightened when the alarm goes off in the morning that he pisses on my leg.

I sometimes worry what it will be like after I've fulfilled my first dream and Vadim is dead.

When I was younger, I thought I wanted to be famous, just like everybody else on the planet. I didn't have anything against the idea of having a well-known mother, either, who smiled from the cover of every magazine and was the talk of the town. But then when we did become known, I could have shot them all—all the photographers and cameramen and the reporters with their microphones and little notepads, filming the entrance to our building and knocking on our neighbors', doors to ask how loud it had been that night. Who screamed, who cried, who ran, and whether Vadim had really said

"There's blood in there, don't go in," and "It's over, get out of here."

Only when one of us emerged—me or Anton, since Alissa still had to be carried then—would they shut their mouths, shuffle to the sides of the hallway to clear a path for us, and watch us pass out of the corners of their eyes.

I had hoped they would try to talk to me or Anton, because then I would have felt justified in knocking the cameras out of their hands or the teeth out of their skulls. But they wisely steered clear of me—there must have been a toxic cloud hanging over me, like Chernobyl. Then again I figured it was probably for the best that they didn't ask me questions and that I didn't react because my mother was always opposed to violence. And she knew exactly what violence felt like.

The next day she was in all the papers. Her first name and the first initial of her last name—as is the journalistic tradition here—along with her age and a photo. It was a picture she'd had taken with her theater group, a nice picture, her hair red, her face less covered with makeup than usual, a black sweater. Back in those days she'd been a star.

Are you happy now? I asked the picture. Didn't I warn you? How could you let this happen? Why did you marry that asshole? Why did he get to come with you to Germany? Why in the hell did you let him into the apartment that night?

Why? For god's sake why?

You were always a stupid, stupid, stupid woman, I said to her. But how could you do this to me—how could you possibly have been so dumb?

Later I apologized to her. Obviously it wasn't her who had done this to me. She had just acted the way she always did—she couldn't help it. She was, after all, an art history student and an artist to boot. She was of an archetype that doesn't really exist anymore—a bit more cosmopolitan, a bit more skilled, a bit more refined. And I'll explain that in my book so everyone knows it. I don't want her to be famous only because she died such a horrid death.

Right from the beginning, I read all the newspaper reports. I would always run down to the newsstand and buy copies of all the papers they sold there. The first few days we weren't at home—the department of family services put us up in an apartment owned by the city. But after two days I told them we couldn't take it anymore. The apartment was completely free of dust, of books, of life. And there was a plastic plant. I said the little kids wanted to go home. It was most important for Alissa. She wasn't even two years old.

We were permitted to go home, where everything was oddly clean in a way it had never been before. We were looked after around the clock by several indistinguishable women with short hair and hyphenated names, and one man with long hair—who also had a hyphenated name.

I can barely remember those days. I just know I talked nonstop about how we had done things *before* and how we needed to keep doing them that way now. How they shouldn't buy any food other than the things we were already used to. Then one day there was organic butter on the table, and I just had a complete breakdown.

I can still remember the look one of the women gave me as I fell screaming to the floor. There was relief in that look. They had been droning on for days about how I didn't need to keep it all inside. How I could give my feelings free rein. Vent. I needed to, in fact.

But I didn't listen to them.

And then suddenly Maria arrived. Cousin twice-removed, with three overstuffed suitcases brought from Novosibirsk. A chance for the *traumatized children* to form a *family* again.

Vadim's cousin, by the way.

I had agreed to her coming—after the experience in the family services-owned apartment, I had an allergic reaction to the idea of entering any kind of institutional facility. And foster parents weren't exactly lined up around the block to take in three emotionally fucked up urchins of Russian origin. Or to move into the apartment where the half-orphans were huddled in the freshly vacuumed corners like frightened rabbits. The apartment with the door that had recently had more pictures snapped of it than Heidi Klum.

So Maria it was.

Maria is in her mid-thirties but looks fifty. She used to work in a factory cafeteria in Novosibirsk. Maria has calloused hands as big as shovels, with nails painted red. She has short hair, dyed blond and permed, thick legs with varicose veins—though you can't see them under the wool stockings she wears. She's got a dozen floral-print dresses, an ass so wide you could land a helicopter on it, perfume so sickly-sweet it makes you sneeze, a big mouth ringed with red lipstick, chipmunk cheeks, and little eyes.

Kind eyes. In fact, she's nice in general, Maria.

Alissa took to her immediately—boom, just like that. Maria this, Maria that. Mascha, mine, ma-ma-ma-Mama. I wasn't upset with her about it—she's just a little kid.

She immediately took up residence in Maria's boundless lap. She wanted to stay there for days on end. It made Maria nervous because she had a hard time cooking with a two-year-old clinging to her. As if any of us wanted to eat. Anton and I didn't eat for days. At some point he basically collapsed—and I piled on.

I told him that if he didn't eat he'd be put in the hospital. And if that happened Maria would be deemed an unfit guardian and sent back to Novosibirsk. And then we'd be stuck in an orphanage or split up and sent out to foster homes alone.

He ate after that. I sat with him and watched him steadily chewing, his big, round eyes fixed on the white wall. Maria kept refilling his plate. Anton threw up twice after eating so I told Maria to stick to smaller portions, but to feed him frequently throughout the day. And not to give him such rich food. And to make sure he drank a lot.

Maria was a good cook. She still is. Much better than my mom. Maria knows how to make borscht and other complicated soups. The apartment always smells like food. She makes homemade stocks from chicken or beef, with vegetables and bundles of soup greens. She makes perfectly shaped meatballs and crepes as thin as cold cuts. She discovered sweetened condensed milk at the Russian grocery store around the corner—a delicacy more prized than caviar during Soviet times—and drenches stacks of crepes in it. She makes homemade pickles and black currant jam.

We're doing well, I tell my mother. We're being fattened up nicely. I wish you could taste it all. You were always intrigued by anything tasty, interesting-looking, or out of the ordinary.

In the newspaper article, Maria was described as "the only living relative willing to look after the three children left behind."

We weren't left behind, I grumbled. And Maria didn't sacrifice some priceless existence for our sake: when you work in a cafeteria in Novosibirsk and you're asked if you'd like to move to Germany to make soup for a few kids, you've hit the lottery.

Particularly since Maria had only briefly been married once when she was young. Maybe twice. She had no kids and no pets—as far as she was concerned there was nothing to tie her to her studio apartment and the cafeteria. That's turned out not to be true. I could have told her so. Back in Novosibirsk she could blather to everyone—and she did. Here she's pretty much damned to silence.

After almost two years here, Maria's German is limited to

about twenty words, things like bus, potato, butter, trash, boil, wash, and fuck you—for the dark-haired teenagers who sometimes whistle and make vulgar gestures at her as she walks past them. Occasionally she tries to group her vocabulary into sentences. That usually doesn't go too well.

When she's shopping anywhere but the Russian grocery store, she has to point to whatever she wants and then write out the number she needs. She always carries a little notepad with her for exactly that purpose. Every time she comes back from the discount market she's bathed in sweat. When she's spoken to on the street, she whimpers and she gets red blotches on her face. I tried for two weeks to help her master the sentence "I only speak Russian." She carries it around on a slip of paper in her wallet, transcribed phonetically into Cyrillic letters.

We're visited regularly by the hyphenated names from the department of family services. Maria freaks out every time, and I have to spend a long time before and after their visits convincing her she is doing a good job and that she won't have to go back to her job in the cafeteria.

Because as unhappy as she is here in the Emerald, you couldn't get her to go back to Novosibirsk—not even by force. She does dream of one day returning there, but later, with a thin waist and fancy makeup, with a suitcase full of nice clothes, and preferably accompanied by a German husband with a perfectly groomed mustache. He should also be kind and rich and speak Russian—because German, Maria says, is tougher than Chinese. As if she knows.

When I do my homework, she sometimes sighs behind me, muttering, "Studying is important, studying is good. I never used to study, always worked. Even as a little kid. And look at me now. Where did all that drudgery get me?"

"Read something, dumpling," I say. "It doesn't have to be *War and Peace* right off the bat. Try a mystery."

"I'm always so tired in the evening, sunshine," she says. "I forget what I've just read and have to keep starting over. It just takes too much effort."

So every day she reads the latest sheet of her page-a-day calendar—one for Russian Orthodox housewives—with a recipe on it, maybe a diet tip, and once in a while a joke, and that suffices. It makes me roll my eyes, but I make sure she doesn't see me. After all, she can't help the fact that she got too few synapses and that she lost two-thirds of the ones she did get working at the cafeteria.

I just worry a little about Alissa. At the moment Maria has a slight intellectual edge over my not quite four-year-old sister, but that won't be the case for long. I have made reading books aloud a mandatory part of Maria's schedule. After the first time she read a picture book to Alissa, she said, amazed, "I never knew such interesting books existed."

She has nothing but love for Alissa. So much so that she was against sending her off to kindergarten at the age of three. She pictured nothing but illnesses and deep-frozen foods. I had to threaten to get the family services department involved to break down Maria's resistance to the idea of kindergarten. She constantly cuddles and pats my sister and can barely keep herself from sputtering the pathetic phrase I've strictly banned from our household: "My poor little orphan." When Alissa's not sitting in her lap, she's standing on a footstool in the kitchen watching meatballs sizzle. She already knows a lot of recipes by heart. Recently she explained to me what fresh cilantro looks like and how it smells. "It makes you want to puke," she said.

Maria's fear of being shipped back to Novosibirsk has a lot to do with Alissa, too. Separating the two of them would not only break my sister's heart but Maria's as well. "When little Ally is all grown up, only then will I feel comfortable leaving," she says. "I want to raise her and make sure she's happy and healthy (my poor little orphan)."

Other times Maria says she'll feel comfortable leaving only once Alissa has found a decent man to marry.

"You're not a servant," I say. "And besides, it's possible she won't find a decent man to marry until she's in her late thirties—if she's lucky."

"Okay, then when she gets her diploma," she says. "That will be a happy day for me, too."

For her "diploma" is a magic term—like "capital gains tax" or "paracetamol."

She would die for Alissa. That's not to say she has anything against Anton. She tries to cuddle him, too, but Anton won't let anyone touch him. He just keeps retreating until his back is against the wall. And at that point Maria realizes she should let go of him. A few months ago I watched as he told Maria about his day at school. She sat at the kitchen table with her chin in her hand shaking her head in amazement.

Maria's afraid of me and that has its advantages.

From her perspective, there are plenty of reasons to be in awe of me. Not only can I speak Latin and French—which are about as relevant to her life as speaking Martian—but I can also speak—and this is something much more concrete—the language in this damn country. I explain the lay of the land to her and take her shopping, where an interpreter comes in very handy. I know how to fill out all the paperwork to apply for welfare and for children's benefits. I'm usually around when workers from the family services department are scheduled to visit. I always offer her the highest praise. When I have to translate a question for her, I always start thinking up the answer to it immediately.

Maria is paralyzed with fear anytime she has to deal with officialdom. Faced with anyone who gives off even a whiff of government authority, she feels as insignificant as an ant. She's even deferential to machines that dispense tickets for the public transportation system. And whenever a plainclothes ticket controller comes through the bus and announces a ticket check, she rushes to rip hers out of her purse so quickly that she sends her lipstick and tampons flying around the nearby seats, an awkward smile plastered on her face all the while.

"Take it easy," I say, if I happen to be there when it happens. Then I crawl around on the floor to collect her things as Maria sits there frozen, the fake smile still on her face after the ticket controller has walked past her.

"I would never have guessed he was a ticket controller," she says, amazed. "With long hair and an earring—like a member of the Beatles. I can't believe the way they are allowed to dress. What did he have hanging from his ears?"

"An MP3 player," I explain.

"A what?"

"For music."

"You're going to be just like your mother," she says one time during an incident like this.

"What did you say?"

She puts her hand over her mouth. She starts to shake, her bloated body quivering beneath her flower-print blouse, terror in her eyes, tears starting to drip down her cheeks—or is it sweat?

"What did you say?"

"Nothing, nothing," she says. "Nothing."

I lift my hand. I'm not sure what I'm about to do. My fingers curl into a fist. But there's no more sense in hitting Maria than in taking a whip to pudding. So I slam my fist against the window.

Nobody turns around. Not even the bus driver, despite the fact that normally they shout at anyone who so much as touches a seat with their foot.

The window doesn't break, but it hurts my fist and I let out a howl.

Suddenly my face is buried in Maria's chest and I can barely breathe. She wraps me up with both arms and also manages to rub my head and back. Her hands feel big and warm.

I close my eyes.

"It's okay," she says as my lungs fill with her perfume. "Everything's going to be fine. Everything is all right. Don't cry, my precious. You're my strong little girl."

"Shut your mouth," I shout, but it comes out as a groan. Maria stops talking.

We get out of the bus downtown to exchange the watch Maria bought two days ago for five euros. It had stopped after one day.

After that I buy a bus ticket for Maria for the return trip and wait as she gets into the bus.

I don't get on with her. Instead I hop on a tram with no ticket—I'm not afraid of the ticket controllers—and go to visit Ingrid and Hans.

It pains me to see their house. I could never tell them why—and wouldn't want to. It's a beautiful two-story house surrounded by a garden that's gone to seed, which would be reason enough to like it.

But what makes visiting them difficult is the fact that my mother loved this house and its garden. She visited it many times, and once, when Ingrid and Hans went to a spa for a month, she and Harry house-sat here together. Actually all of us moved in here for those four weeks—my mother, me, Anton, and Alissa. And Harry, who beamed during those weeks in a way he never did otherwise. We were all his guests, sort of, and hosting us made him proud.

Of course, it wasn't really his home anymore. Finally, in his early thirties he had managed to move out of his parents' place. Must have been about a year and a half before he met my mother. After he left home he lived in a studio apartment in a student neighborhood—a fourth-floor walkup. I went there twice. It was a nice little place.

Both times I visited were a bit stressful, though, because Harry was ashamed of the place and spent the whole time apologizing for everything—for the fact that his kitchen was messy and because he had run out of coffee, for the pair of underpants lying on the floor. He seemed particularly bothered about the underpants on the floor. I told him a thousand times I didn't care, that I was used to much worse. But his embarrassment didn't subside for the rest of the time I was there. It didn't help that my mother couldn't stop laughing.

She sat on a chair and laughed at everything: Harry scrambling to scoop up his underpants and shove them into a drawer only to have paperwork fly out of the drawer, me tripping over his sneakers, Harry knocking over bottles as he tried to find cookies in the kitchen. I didn't think she should laugh so loudly—it just made poor Harry blush, leaving him even more embarrassed. I even told her that—in Russian—but she just brushed me off and said I didn't know anything. As Harry ran around, she followed him with her gaze, and there was tenderness and affection in her look.

Harry didn't speak to her at all during that visit. He was too busy trying to make sure I was happy, despite the fact that I didn't need anything. He looked intently at my face, searching for any sign of an emotion that might spell trouble for him, and occasionally turned to my mother to give her a look or a shy smile.

I sat on his couch, drank rose hip tea—which I can't stand—and nibbled on stale cookies, trying as best I could to seem comfortable so he would settle down. At some point he finally did. He stopped running around and sat down next to me. He told me about his studies and whatever job he was doing then—which, it goes without saying, wasn't going well.

He was exactly as my mother had described. A little difficult to be around at first because he was so unsure of himself. But as he gained confidence, he was kind and thoughtful.

"So?" my mother asked as we were winding our way down the stairs toward the door of his building.

"He's definitely okay," I said. "You can bring him over to our place."

"He's a prince among men," she said. She hadn't worried at all about what I would think of him. Unlike him, she was usually sure of herself.

"I could never go to bed with a guy like that," I said gruffly to counter the uncharacteristically warm feeling the meeting had left me with. A lover who got on well with his new girlfriend's kids was not part of the usual drill. "He's kind of frantic."

"I don't think he'd be into you either," said my mother, with a bit of venom.

"Do you find him at all handsome?" I asked.

My mother huffed.

"Tell him he should do something else with his hair," I grumbled.

"Tell him yourself," she muttered. "Tell him exactly how he should do it."

"Then he'll be insulted. And he wouldn't listen to me anyway."

"You're wrong there."

And she was right.

He never moved in with us because our place was too small. But he slept there regularly. His toothbrush stayed in the bathroom and his slippers under the coat rack in the hall. He kept his robe in my mother's closet. And I had no qualms about using the hair gel he did in fact buy on my advice and stored in our bathroom.

He looked really cute once he stopped parting his hair. Light brown hair sticking up, funny eyes, a bashful grin. Alissa loved him, as did Anton—Anton most of all, in fact. A man who practically lived here, helped with the dishes, never shouted, held hands with mom and played memory games with the kids, a man who listened, buttered our bread for us, and happily stepped in as a babysitter if anything ever came up.

And yet still not a man Anna would go for.

Because he was a loser—and that's just an objective fact. He was one because he felt like one. He had studied literature for twelve years and was still no closer to finishing his degree. He bounced from job to job because he wasn't cutthroat enough to succeed at anything. He'd lived too long with his parents—even by local standards. He mumbled. And whenever he was nervous or unsure of himself—which was almost all the time—he talked so hurriedly and unclearly that you always had to ask him to repeat whatever he said. Which would in turn startle him and he'd start to stutter.

When I was younger, I would never have believed a German man like this existed. So meek, so helpless. Never thinking of himself. Broke but still generous. Instead of a driver's license a rickety girl's bike. In his checkered shirt and bowl cut—until he met me, that is.

My mother's great love.

I never asked either of them, but I am sure she was Harry's first. At most his second. He was seven years younger than she was and would have been more inexperienced even if he'd lived two hundred years. What sane woman would take up with someone who was the very embodiment of helplessness? My mother. Nobody else would. I could certainly never imagine myself with someone like that.

But I could understand what my mother liked about him.

He was the exact opposite of Vadim, who left two and a half nervous wrecks behind when he finally moved out. My mother, Anton, and little Alissa. I was not a nervous wreck. I was a simmering cauldron of hatred. Once he was gone, my mother popped a bottle of champagne and she and I clinked glasses—her hand was shaking and she had tears in her eyes.

"I'm lucky," she said. "I've got a chance to really do some living now." And she did start living, and she bumped into Harry. She met him in the offices of the little local paper in which her column on Russian-Germans appeared. She would write pieces on things like the fact that you could get Russian-language books at the local library, or that there was story time there every Thursday, or that there were cheap gymnastics classes available somewhere. She approached the column with real devotion. She liked helping those who were less knowledgeable or less capable than she was. She ran our phone number in the paper for anyone who had questions—and the phone rang a lot.

My mother was very proud of that job. Next to each of her columns was a small photo of her, and she could never get used to seeing her name and face in print. The fact that the paper had a circulation of five thousand and was filled for the most part with ads for plumbers and beer gardens didn't bother her. She sat and worked on her articles for hours, agonizing over each phrase, only to have me proofread everything and change it all around again.

Harry was freelancing for the paper too. It was his latest job. He had just failed miserably as a waiter. The paper paid about ten cents a line and nobody who thought anything of themselves would write for that rate. Before Harry and my mother showed up, the only writers had been officers of sports clubs who wrote up pieces on things like their clubs' end-of-season banquets—they would have paid to have their stuff published.

I'm thinking about all of this as I ring the bell at Ingrid and Hans's front gate. It takes a while before the door opens and Ingrid steps out into the yard, squinting and unsure, blinded by the sun.

"Sascha?" she says when she finally hits upon the idea of using her hand to shield her eyes and is able to see me. "What a pleasant surprise. Come in, my child."

I walk across the moss-covered cobblestones that lead from the gate to the door. I had told her I was coming a week ago. Ingrid must have forgotten—but she's always home anyway.

She wraps her arms around me and holds me close for a long time—until my back starts to hurt. She's short and I have to stoop.

When she lets go, I can see in her face that she's trying to suppress sobs. She's not able to. I don't look away. I'm feeling tired and indifferent. I don't cry, either. I'm not sure why Ingrid does.

"This is going to make Hans happy," she whispers. "How nice of you to come see us again."

She quickly puts on a pot of coffee and sets the table in the living room. It's become routine for me to eat in the living room. There's almost nothing that can shock me these days. Ingrid has discreetly wiped the tears away with a cloth handkerchief—as if she could hide something like that from me—and returns upbeat, almost cheerful. She fumbles awkwardly with the coffee cups and they clink against one another, and all the while she smiles at me with Harry's smile. I think she's even humming a melody.

The smell of the coffee fills the air.

"Hans, Hans," she calls, a little louder than necessary. "Can you look to see whether we have any cake in the freezer? The one with the crumb topping? Or the cheesecake?"

"Please don't go to any trouble," I mutter, but she doesn't pay any attention. Which is fine.

"Sugar, cream," she says, setting down the jar of sugar and a creamer on the table. She puts them right in front of me, as if I'm the only one who will be having anything. "How are your little sister and brother, my child? How's their health?"

"Anton's never healthy," I say, regretting it immediately as I see the look on her face darken. Her question wasn't just small talk. Her gloominess had been lifted for a moment by my visit, but it disturbs deeply her to hear about an unhealthy child. When someone hurts, Ingrid hurts with them. She can't watch the news without crying.

"Nothing serious," I say. "Just nerves—just psychological."

"Psychological," she repeats. "That's the most serious of all, my child."

I don't contradict her. But that stuff has never been an issue for me. A Russian children's poem comes to mind: "My nerves are made of steel, no, actually I don't have any at all." It's like it was written about me. I don't have any.

I wonder whether I should tell Ingrid that I want to kill Vadim. Maybe it'll cheer her up the way it did me and Anton.

Hans comes through the door.

He's friendly as he greets me, but seems emotionally distant. He holds my hand in his for a long time. I've stood up from my chair to greet him and it has apparently surprised him. He's a bit unsteady on his feet, though he's not really that old. Not even sixty, I don't think. He's become grizzled. The skin of his face hangs in flabby folds.

He tries to put on a smile, but what he musters is more of a horrible grimace. It pains me to look at him. I would like to tell him he doesn't need to smile on my account, but I can't think of how to say it.

We have coffee and a crumb cake Ingrid has thawed in the microwave. For the first fifteen minutes Ingrid talks nonstop. It's all a bit muddled: geraniums, the neighbors, water pipes, a broken vacuum cleaner. I nod throughout. Then she stops. We sit there silently. The clock ticks. It seems quite natural to me.

Hans has a faraway look on his face, Ingrid stirs her coffee, and I look at the photos on the walls. I'm already pretty familiar with them. All shots of Harry, or nearly all, at least. Harry as a boy, with matted blond hair and freckles. Harry with a wiener dog. Harry in a sun hat, sitting in the passenger seat of an antique car. Harry building a sand castle. Harry with his book bag. Harry with a young Ingrid and Harry with a young Hans. In a tender hug with his mom, looking serious standing stiffly next to his father.

Harry as a child, but never with friends. Or girlfriends. In a lounge chair, in the woods, on a bike. A portrait of a somewhat older Harry. White teeth and freckles. A good photo.

How can something like that happen, I think to myself. Harry had loving parents, a sheltered childhood in a prosperous country, a dog, a house with a garden. This house, where I am sitting right now. And yet Harry was unhappy, because he was never any good at anything. What did his parents do wrong—were they just too nice to him?

If I had grown up here, I would be a completely different person, I think. I wouldn't be so combative and I probably wouldn't be so obsessed about my grades in school—especially in subjects I'm not interested in, like medieval history. I would have been born to succeed, and I wouldn't have to bust my ass all the time just trying to prove to everyone that I'm a somebody.

At the Alfred Delp School they wouldn't risk snickering about me behind my back or scrutinizing my no-name sneakers out of the corners of their eyes. I would be somebody. Even if I wore the exact same shoes I do now—it just wouldn't matter.

I'd be easygoing, fearless, and nonchalant.

Okay, I'm like that now, too. But then I'd be confident, too.

To my right, at the farthest end of the wall, is a photo I haven't seen before. I can't quite make it out. I squint. Ingrid and Hans don't notice—they've probably forgotten I'm here.

I push my chair back and stand up. I walk over to the picture and about halfway there I recognize it and stop abruptly.

It's a photo I took. With Harry's new digital camera. At our place, on the balcony. It's the only picture on the wall with a few people in it besides Harry—all of three people, all together with

Harry. My mother, around whose shoulder he has one of his arms. Alissa, who is balanced on his right knee and my mother's left. And Anton, who is sitting next to Harry, squeezed up against him on the narrow bench.

It's pretty stupid to stand in the middle of a room and stare at a wall. I must have been standing here like this for quite a while. Ingrid and Harry have come to and turn their heads toward me.

"What happened, my child," asks Ingrid, unsettled. "What is it? What are you looking at? Why are you crying?"

There is no sense in telling her I'm not crying.

Ingrid squints, too, and peers in the direction I'm staring. Then she realizes what I'm looking at.

"You're sad because you're not there? Not in the picture? Is that it?"

Ingrid gets up and hurries over to me, but then stops and stands just behind me, unsure of herself.

I shake my head and head back to the table. Ingrid follows me.

"We didn't find any shots of you on his camera," says Hans. They're the first words I've heard out of his mouth today. "There were only a couple of pictures on it—it was brand new."

I know. I showed Harry how it worked.

"Give us a picture of you, my child. We meant to ask you for one anyway."

I shake my head again.

"Why not? Do you have any nice big ones? I'll buy a pretty frame for it."

I jump up, excuse myself, and run to the bathroom. I know where everything is in this house. From the bathroom window I can look out at the lush garden, rustling in the breeze. All the way at the back is an apple tree. The apples on it always ripen early and seem to glow milky white from the inside. I can hear

Ingrid and Hans's flustered voices from the living room. I bite my lip for a few minutes, then flush the toilet and give my hands a good wash.

"I'll wrap up some cake for you to take home, okay?" says Ingrid.

I don't tell her that Maria bakes a cake every other day and that I can't stand cake.

I clear my throat and say, "That would be nice."

"But you'll stay for a bit longer, won't you, my child? I know it must be boring for you here. We don't want to keep you."

"Unfortunately I've got to get going."

"You could do your homework here sometime."

I look at Ingrid, stunned. Her suggestion doesn't make any sense to me.

"We've got lots of books, and Hans could help you," she says. "He knows a lot."

Hans isn't listening. If he were, he would have contradicted her.

I stifle a grin and thank them for having me.

When Ingrid goes into the kitchen to get some tin foil, I decide to try a little shock therapy.

"Hans," I say quietly, "you know what, Hans? I'm going to kill him."

Hans looks at me.

"I'm going to kill Vadim."

"Vadim?" he says, struggling to repeat after me.

"Yes, Vadim. The murderer. I'm going to murder the murderer."

He looks at me.

"Just like in the Old Testament. An eye for an eye and a tooth for a tooth. Justice."

"Vadim who?" Hans asks, his voice a bit hoarse.

"There's no way you could have forgotten Vadim, Hans. I'm going to avenge them. My mother and Harry."

Hans looks at me. I can't read his facial expression at all. He's just completely blank. He doesn't say a word.

I want to smack myself. What got into you, you stupid cow, I think.

If my words even registered with Hans, he still won't believe them. I wonder what he will think when he hears I've actually pulled it off? Will he come back to life, if just for a second? Will he feel a sense of satisfaction? Something even approaching happiness? Will his eyes light up? Will Ingrid's?

She comes back in and slides a silvery package into my hand.

"Don't crush it—that's the cake," she says earnestly.

"Thanks," I say. "I'll call you again soon."

I start to turn the door handle and feel Ingrid's hand on mine. Her touch is cold and fleeting. I open my fist and find a 50 euro bill that wasn't there before.

"Please take it, child. We have no use for our money anyway. Buy something for the little ones. You have such a good heart."

I stick the bill into my jeans pocket. Ingrid looks almost happy. I bet she's wondering now whether I would have accepted more. I was expecting her to do this since I didn't turn down the money last time. Right before that last time, Ingrid told me how sad it was not to have anyone to give gifts to.

"If you ever need anything . . . " Ingrid says.

"I'll holler," I say as I hop out onto the walkway before Ingrid can think to hug me goodbye.

In the tram I press my forehead to the window. I shouldn't fool myself—there's no way Ingrid and Hans are going to be excited about my plan. They're not like Anton.

They're going to be appalled. Horrified. They are nice and naïve. They can never understand why unemployment is so high or why some people take drugs and others leave their newborn babies in dumpsters. They'll be just as mystified at the fact that the girl they used to slip money and cake to could kill another human being. Or rather, an inhuman being.

They'd probably be hurt if I stepped on a dog's paw in their presence. They consider the fact that their son will never return some kind of inexplicable, nightmarish misunderstanding. That's why ever since it happened they've been operating in a dreamlike haze. At first they seemed to be counting on waking up one day and finding everything back the way it had always been. Then at some point they resigned themselves to the fact that there was no way out of this nightmare.

But since they don't read the papers anymore and don't talk to anybody, maybe they wouldn't even find out I'd killed him. If they're even still alive then.

Don't know whether you can even say they are alive now.

Anyway, I'm not ready to do it yet. Logistically speaking.

I have a bunch of books on criminology at home. But so far they haven't inspired the perfect plan yet. Sometimes I imagine breaking a bottle over Vadim's head. But I'm pretty sure that wouldn't kill him—it would just get his blood all over me. And that's not enough. Not for me. No way.

Then I think of a heavy object—an iron or a dumbbell. In old mysteries they always talk about candlesticks, and we have one of those at home that would do the trick. From the flea market.

That could work. Here's the scenario: Vadim comes to visit, to see Alissa and Anton. As usual—like he always used to before—he brings chocolate. "I'll make us some tea," I say helpfully, "and you can tell us about prison." Vadim sits down at the table with his back to me, waiting for his tea. That was something he always used to do, too. He always sat and waited for things—a plate of pickled herring, a pen, a clean shirt.

I hate men. All of them except Anton.

Then the moment would come. Finally. Yes.

The spot where Vadim had just a moment before had a head would be reduced to nothing more than a bloody mush. A bit of a shame that it would drip on our table and floor. Maybe I'll put down a tarp. I'm not sure whether I'll say anything as I do it: "This is for my mother and Harry," for instance. Or, "Drop dead." But hang on, this isn't a soap opera I'm planning here. I just want to get it done. No need to sing a song or recite a poem.

And by the way, that's not how it's going to go. Anton and Alissa can't be there. Especially not Anton. Once is enough. I'll tell Vadim that the kids are on their way home and will be right there. That he should have a seat so I can bring him a cup of tea.

His kids. That's what they used to be. Now they're mine.

Shooting him would also work. But I have to be realistic. The chances of me getting hold of a gun are slim. Though it would be appropriate. Vadim had a pistol for years. Anna says guns are just a way to compensate for a small cock. It's the best line I've ever heard come out of her mouth.

Back in the army, a hundred years ago, Vadim was supposed to have been a pretty good shot. He loved to talk about it whenever he couldn't understand something he got in the mail from the authorities, or when he couldn't find any clean socks, or when my mother went out at night without him, ignoring his tantrum. At those moments he would talk about the army and his face would get all pensive. "Back in the army," he would say, "we skewered the bastards on the bayonets of our AK-47s."

Anton shivered and didn't ask what Vadim meant by that.

In the final stretch, before Vadim moved out, Anton often shook with fear in his presence. And never opened his mouth. Sometimes I thought he had completely lost the ability to speak. It didn't surprise me at all that his teacher kept asking our mother to come in for parent-teacher conferences to discuss the fact that Anton "refused to participate"—as she put it in the letters she sent home—in class discussions.

If he hadn't continued to show "good effort" in his written work—even "very good" sometimes—the teacher would probably have just tolerated a student who sat pale and silently in the back row, barely distinguishable from the wall. But she was a young teacher, and still cared about her students. She wanted to find out why when this kid in her class was spoken to he would just clamp his mouth shut and refuse eye contact as adamantly as he refused to speak. So she tormented Anton with unusually determined efforts to engage with him, and my mother with invitations to come in to talk about the problem.

The first one was actually a *parents*-teacher conference. Both of Anton's parents went. Vadim let my mother tie his tie for him, but he kept swatting her hands away impatiently. My mother wasn't as good at tying a tie as Anton was at his written school work.

A steady stream of comments came from Vadim, too. Like, "I keep asking myself if maybe they switched the arms and legs when they were putting you together." And, "Quit yanking me all around, you idiot." And, "Why can't you just tie the fucking thing?" And, "You are the most useless woman I've ever met." And, "Get it done—how many years am I supposed to wait around while you figure it out?"

Through all of this I was doing my homework at the kitchen table. Actually I wasn't doing my homework because I was sitting there in a helpless rage, my fist clenched around my pen. I wasn't upset at Vadim but at my mother—a situation I found myself in a lot back then.

If someone did that to me, I'd pull the stupid tie until his throat started to rattle. Then I'd go into the kitchen and put the kettle on. And before he had a chance to loosen the noose and catch his breath, I'd go back in and pour boiling water over his head. That's the bare minimum someone who talked to me that way could reckon with.

And what do you do, I thought, scrawling angry, jagged lines across my binder. You don't say a thing. You let yourself get pushed away and smile, lost in your own thoughts. You go back to helping him if he asks you to, and you even keep helping him when he viciously insults you. With the patience of an angel, you let yourself get walked all over—you, of all people. You, a person who takes such pride in being courteous to everyone around you.

It pains me that you almost always remain civil. And I know it's not because you're afraid of him. You don't even see him anymore, you don't hear him. You couldn't care less about him—and for that you feel bad. Despite what he's like.

You don't take him seriously at all. You let him rage and scream at you and tell you you're not allowed to do things—things you'll obviously do anyway. You let him blather on about things he doesn't have a clue about, which is pretty much everything except his glory days back in the army and the exact mechanical workings of our toilet.

You don't react when he spews his hateful tirades about the fucking Germans, who can't manage their own country, the fucking Americans, who try to worm their way into everything like members of the biggest cult in the world, the fucking Italians, who talk so damn fast. About the Russian mobsters who turn their backs on their own country and about the Russian morons who don't. About the fucking job placement office, which is never able to find the right job for such a world-class professional like Vadim. And about his piece-of-shit boss who dared to make a stupid comment—just too stupid for Vadim to take, too stupid for him to be able to stay on the job, making that piece of shit the only boss he's ever had here, and for only a short time at that.

And first and foremost, over and over, about fucking

women. About the German women, who wear the ugliest clothes on earth, don't shave their legs, and have the gall to earn more in a month than Vadim has in his entire life. And French women, sluts every one—even the way they talk sounds slutty, as if they all just want to be laid down and nailed. Turkish women, so disgustingly fat beneath the tents they wear, pumping out a new baby every year, drinking tea with their husbands' other wives, and speaking German worse than Vadim himself.

And about the Russian women, stupid and ugly, with vulgar taste in clothing, who think they can talk and laugh around Vadim with their backs to him, as if he weren't even there. Of all people, they are best equipped to understand and appreciate Vadim's unique qualities but—damn them!—they simply refuse to do so.

And then there's this one here, the one he took pity on and married despite the fact that she had an insufferable, illegitimate freak of a daughter on her hip. The one he generously gave two more kids—kids who didn't fucking appreciate him nearly enough. Instead of listening to him ramble on for hours, they pored through pointless books by moronic writers. Instead of polishing Vadim's shoes, the girls teach his son how to play chess. Instead of cooking, they cackle on the telephone with their friends. Whenever Vadim's on his deathbed with the flu, they make tea with lemon for him, sure, but they sing as they do. As if it's all fun and games.

She acts in plays and gets applause. Her picture appears in the paper. People approach her on the street. The phone is constantly ringing. Always for her, only her. Nobody ever wants to talk to Vadim. And if they do, it's only about one thing: "your wife this," "your Marina that."

She shouldn't think as a result that she's somehow better than him. Under no circumstances should she ever be permitted to think she married an old, useless sack of shit, which is how he sometimes feels about himself as he sits in front of the television morning, noon, and night, watching all those idiots who just waste Vadim's valuable time—and get paid to do it.

To make sure she never thinks that way, she can't be told often enough who she really is: a useless wife who can't run the household or make decent money running around at what she calls a job but that doesn't seem fit to be called work at all.

An uncaring mother who doesn't iron her kids' T-shirts, who has nothing against her kids making a mess doing arts and crafts or playing, who doesn't care whether their hair is neatly cut—especially the one who is supposed to be a man. I should pull your hair right out myself; I'm sure everyone makes fun of you at school.

A chaotic woman whose bureau is always messy and who can't manage to have meals ready on time. No wonder the children are so directionless. They think they're allowed to do whatever they want. Like yelling and screaming inside the apartment when Vadim is trying to watch TV.

And a whore who can get herself off with a vibrator as if it were the real deal. Who goes out to the movies at night without her husband, who dyes her hair and wears it down. Who dresses as if she had a nice figure—maybe the Turks are onto something after all with their full-body curtains.

You let him say all of this, you let him show all his disgust, I think bitterly, and the most you ever do is shrug your shoulders. Your most extreme facial expression is nothing more than a look of bottomless sorrow. Instead of thinking how to save yourself, you think about how to save *him* before he goes over the edge. You're worried he'll start to drink. You just don't understand that his survival instinct is stronger than yours.

You raise your voice only when he turns from you to the children. That's his biggest weapon. He knows that's the only way he can really hurt you. And that's the only time you will strike back. When he's shouting at Anton, he knows your broken-voiced threat to divorce him is serious. So usually he does that only at home. Anton is about as capable of defending himself as the little lemon tree on the windowsill. And he makes just as frail an impression as it does.

I'm not sure the extent of the daily hell Anton experiences—Vadim holds back when I'm around and Anton never talks about it. The most common word I use around Vadim is "police." And even though he always laughs, I can see the fear and doubt in his eyes.

But he also knows I don't want to hurt you. It's a perennial woman's mistake: I don't want to cause you pain, so I allow you to be killed. I never do go to the police—in part because Vadim always pulls himself together around me, but mostly because I know you would never approve of it except in the most dire situation.

You hope everything will somehow work out. One time you tell me you dream of him leaving on his own after he falls in love with someone new. Otherwise, you feel like you'd be kicking someone when he's down. If somebody is on the ground, you can't kick them. Just another one of the many noble but hollow rules you live by. When you tell me this, I have to laugh, long and sinister, until I start to cry. I'll never forget the look on your face at that moment.

You'll never know why for years I left my room only once I was fully clothed, never in pajamas or a bathrobe. Or why I locked the door to my room at night, and why only now can I wear short sleeves or anything else remotely revealing. You always called me "buttoned up," even "prudish." You accepted it as my own peculiarity, and I never let on that there was something else behind it. I thought it would hurt you, that you wouldn't be able to take it, that you would snap from the guilt and horror.

Which means I enabled you to remain blind to him.

Among the happiest moments of my life with Vadim were the victories I scored on the battlefield, little personal victories that affected only me. The look on his face when I kicked him—I could see the debate raging in his hate-filled eyes as he weighed whether to keep it up or to hit me back. Because that might leave clues I might not stay quiet about. I could see his fear as I sat at the kitchen table slowly turning the bread knife in my fingers and staring at him. And I could feel him slowly pull his knee away from mine under the table.

But maybe I'm lying to myself, and the victory was really his. His triumph that I never left my laundry or any personal items in the bathroom and that I kept everything locked in my room. That I steered clear of him, meaning I spent almost all of my time at home in my room. And that I never said a word about any of it to my mother.

I feel so horribly guilty thinking that maybe my silence was the railroad switch that sent the train onto the wrong track, headed for death.

He who shoots gets shot, I think. How simple and just.

It warms my heart.

I still have a lot to read, I think. Read and study and think. He mustn't stand a chance. No way to defend himself and no way to live through it.

These are nice thoughts, but they're taxing. I should spend some time on the other plan.

I sit down that same night at the computer. I sit there for a long time, at least an hour. It's harder than I thought it would be. It'll probably be easier to strangle Vadim.

All the scenes I want to write down seem to have vanished. Every syllable I try to capture seems banal. Warm hands and lullabies and dirty jokes and coffee by the liter—none of it hits the mark. All I can see is her face in my mind, and I begin to type just to avoid staring like Anton.

"Red hair," I write. "Dyed with henna as long as I can

remember. What color was her hair before that? Probably some shade of brown. She once told me she found her first gray hair early. By the time she was thirty she had skeins of gray hair. She had the type of life that makes people prematurely gray. With the henna, her gray hair became streaks of light orange. Her eyes were light brown and big. Her mouth was big, too, and, like her eyes, was usually wide open. She talked and laughed a lot. Even when she read, she talked. She would always show up in front of me with a book in her hand and say, 'Should I read a passage to you? Here's an incredible paragraph.' I would answer, 'I'm doing my homework,' or, 'I'm trying to read something of my own.' She read the passage anyway, and I never understood what was so great about it. I never really listened because it annoyed me and I was happier lost in my own thoughts."

I read through it again. I don't cry.

I go to bed early.

In the morning I put on my sneakers with my eyes still closed. Maria is snoring loudly in her bed, and when I go to close her door so she doesn't wake up the children, I see little Alissa next to her, half buried by Maria's overflowing hips. Alissa's in a hand-made floral nightgown. Memories of a pink sweater shoot through my head and I decide I need to do something about organizing the clothes.

Maria listens to me.

I run three times around the Emerald and then head off. I'm dragging. I haven't run in a long time and wouldn't have today if I hadn't woken up with a sick, tense feeling. I try to run away from this feeling but just end up with stitches in my sides. So I shove my hands under my ribs and stand there wheezing in front of the newsstand.

I've had a subscription to the local paper for the past year. I need to. If the Emerald were being torn down, for instance, Maria would probably only realize when they carried her out of the apartment in her chair. And anyway, reading the paper often pays off for school.

I look at the headlines of the dailies, more out of a sense of duty than out of real interest.

I wonder to myself who in this area buys these. Sometimes I feel like the only literate person in the entire Emerald. The rest of them carry half-empty bottles around in the pockets of their track pants, wrap smoked fish in bright-colored papers with headlines like "Who does the severed head belong to?" or "Government covers up evidence of another UFO landing," and look suspiciously at anyone who uses German to speak to them. "Can't he speak normal?" they ask.

On this morning, my heart suddenly freezes—just for a second—then it kicks on again and jumps into my throat and flutters there like a bird in distress. I gasp for breath and try to swallow in order to get my heart back down where it belongs.

As I do this, I move closer so I can read a box in which one of the big Frankfurt papers highlights the main stories of the day. Under "local" I read: "A visit with the double-murderer Vadim E: 'remorse is tearing my heart apart.'"

His heart, my heart, I think. Maybe it would be a good idea to tear that organ right out of his chest and impale it on a spear for all to see. Actually I get queasy easily. I don't like to watch when Maria guts a chicken and explains how you have to cut the oil gland off the back of the bird and how the part with the eggs is the ovaries. And how if you hold a severed chicken foot and pull the tendon in the front, the claws will make a fist—what's so disgusting about that, sweetie?

But for this one thing, I could get past any hang-ups.

My running pants don't have any pockets. No pockets on the jacket either. Otherwise I wouldn't have my keys dangling from my neck, jangling like a cowbell.

I have to read what's in the paper right this second. In the amount of time it would take me to go upstairs and get money, the world could end. Five times.

I look over at one of the Emerald's second-floor windows. Normally there'd be a bald head sticking out of it, with an unlit, saliva-soaked cigarette stuck in the corner of its mouth.

There's nobody in the window. It's still really early, and any sensible person who has to be awake at this hour is making a cup of coffee right about now. Or a second cup.

All I can think is how glad I am Ingrid and Hans don't see me grab the paper, roll it up, and tuck it under my jacket.

On the staircase I open it up again and flip through it looking for the article about the woes of the aging Vadim E.

The first thing that catches my eye is the byline—Susanne Mahler. She's the writer. Only after that do I see the grotesque face. The sight of it makes me feel faint.

I lean my head against the dirty green wall. A little higher up on the wall is a scribbled drawing, a detailed image of two men copulating. My head leans against the caption: "Death to all faggots." I take a few deep breaths. Then I look at the paper again.

He hasn't changed. The same mustache, the same dark eyes, the same hulking brow and deep creases running from the sides of his nose to the corners of his mouth. The ugliest face I've ever seen, made even worse by the pitiful expression he's put on for the photo. The corners of his mouth hang sadly, his eyes plead, his curly hair is sticking up all crazy. Poor Vadim. He barks, but he doesn't bite—unless someone is so mean as to bait him. Then he'll snap at you, of course, but it's your own fault for getting him worked up. As long as you know how to behave around him, he's a sweetheart.

Everything goes black again. This time I have to take deliberate breaths for much longer before the darkness starts to dissipate.

He probably weaseled his way in with my mother with that pitiful grimace, I think to myself. Playing to her empathetic soul. She petted anyone who looked up at her like that. Dogs, too—and not one of them ever bit her.

But she sure as hell got suckered by Vadim. How could she have been so stupid? Couldn't she see what a monster he was right away?

"He used to be different," my mother said to me once. "Not so angry and so weak. You know yourself how bad it's gotten since he began spending all day in front of the TV, barely understanding a word."

"I know exactly what he was like before, too. And it wasn't any better."

"That's not fair."

"And what about him? Is he fair?"

"He's having a hard time, you can see that yourself."

Be careful of people who feel weak, I think. Because it's possible that one day they'll want to feel strong and you'll never recover from it. Maybe that's a thought to add to my file, the one I'm going to call "Marina." The stuff I wrote last night I deleted immediately afterwards.

I can't get over the feeling that Susanne Mahler wants to pet Vadim E. a little.

I have to read the piece a dozen times. And even then I don't really understand it. Individual sentences stick out in my head and mix with others. *I still love her. I wish I could tell her. I'm writing her a letter. It's already 20 pages long, but the most important thing hasn't been said yet. I'm ashamed to face my children. I'm also terribly sorry about the young man who also had to die.*

The only thing that's yours is a prison cell, I mutter. In a million years, I would never believe you said all of that on your own. Maybe Susanne Mahler took an interpreter with her who did as creative a job of translating as I do for Maria?

*I've become a completely different person. Even my German is improving.*

Susanne Mahler seems touched by it all. She looked at Vadim's sketches—his attempts to hang onto the image of his wife's transcendent beauty. His ex-wife, to be more precise. Whom he unfortunately killed—which perhaps he shouldn't have done.

*The drawings are primitive but heartfelt and expressive*, according to Susanne Mahler.

My whole body is shaking with rage.

Vadim would be happy to show the letter he wrote to his wife to anybody who is interested. Susanne Mahler had held the handwritten pages in her hand; unfortunately she can't read Russian.

The script is erratic, inconsistent, agitated.

Vadim has many more years to continue writing. I start to laugh. Vadim is writing about my mother. We're rivals.

It would be better if instead he'd just kill himself. Or maybe not. I still hope to accomplish something in life.

I fold the paper, roll it up, and head upstairs. I carefully open the door and take off my shoes. For a second I think I see a ghost. But it's only Maria in her flowing nightgown, made from the same fabric as Alissa's.

Maria sews, too. Have I mentioned that?

She jumps when our eyes meet.

"Did you fall?" she asks and squints intently at my face. Her own face is swollen and pale like bread dough. Her cheeks quiver when she moves. She has pink and blue curlers in her hair.

A dream woman.

"Good morning," I say, and walk past her to the bathroom.

I won't say a word to her about it. She's never mentioned Vadim in front of me. It's wise of her. I know they barely saw each other. She visited us once, at most, while we were still in Moscow. I don't know what she thinks of him and I don't want to know.

I've never asked her what she thinks of my plan. It's never occurred to me. I want to believe that she might sigh but that she wouldn't say anything—and that she'd help me clean up the mess before the children got home.

She would understand that more blood wouldn't be helpful for their development.

I also want to be sure that when it comes to bringing up the children, she'll stick to my handbook while I'm in prison. Where perhaps Susanne Mahler will visit me and report: *Sascha N. seems very much at peace. "I would do it all again," she told this reporter, "if I hadn't already succeeded in poisoning Vadim . . ."*

I update and expand my educational handbook regularly. As of now, it consists of the following:

1. Your mother was the best ever, and she lives on in you.

2. The idea that Vadim is your father is a big misunderstanding. Sascha believes that you are not his children but rather the children of the pilot who lived one floor down—a wonderful and handsome man. That's why you are so good-looking.

3. Read everything you can get your hands on. That's what your mother did.

4. Learn everything you want to know, and then learn some more. Don't worry if something doesn't go well. You are capable of so much.

5. Even if Maria likes to tell you the opposite, it doesn't matter what other people think of you. Wear whatever you feel like, dye your hair blue if you think it looks nice. Act however you want, too.

6. Sing a lot.

7. Watch out for people who feel weak. They may want to feel strong one day and you might not survive that moment.

8. Don't put any credence in worst-case scenarios like the one in the previous entry, even if Maria constantly predicts the

end of the world is right around the corner. Be courageous and crazy and explore every wonderland you come across—just like Alice in the English fairytale, after whom your mother named Alissa.

9. Think about your older sister Sascha once in a while. But don't visit her in prison—it's not good for the psyche.

10. You are not poor little orphans, because your mother is immortal. Maria knows that, too.

And then I realize I don't know anything about what Maria knows or doesn't know.

I skip out of school two hours early one day because I just can't take it anymore. I've felt for days as if I were wandering around in a thick, gray fog. I recognize the world around me, but it's lost all color. I just don't feel like looking any closer.

I don't hear things around me—or to put it more accurately, I'm not listening, and the voices around me are blurred into a tangled rush of noise. The only thing I react to are children's shrieks. I always turn to look to make sure it's not Anton or Alissa. At home I spend most of my time lying in bed.

I've blown two exams—history and math. In both cases, the teachers came up to me after the class and said they wouldn't count the exams toward my midterm grade. I didn't understand what they were talking about at first because I hadn't even opened the test booklet in either case.

I didn't look at the teachers. I can't stand those eyes. Another set of eyes examining me with worry and sympathy. Following me when I leave. I don't want that.

I want to be invisible. But my mother wouldn't have liked that. She always said you should be able to see, hear, and smell people.

I'm sure everyone would happily smell a little less of people than they have to smell of Vadim, I always answered. Is he allergic to water?

Once when I was a little kid I was bored in school and just got up and walked out of class, my mother told me.

I'm not bored now. But I leave two hours early because I'm afraid of just turning to stone in my chair. Unlike Anton, I don't have an older sister to drag me back into the land of the living.

I am the older sister.

I ride the tram toward home in a fog. My sneakers dangle from my backpack, tied together by the laces. The rolled-up newspaper is stuck in the side pocket.

The heater is going underneath my seat. I can't bring myself to switch seats.

But I'm roasting, so I manage to do something else: pull out the paper and open it. I always carry the entire paper around rather than just pulling out the local section. Just how I do it. The pages are frayed and falling apart.

I look at Vadim's picture several times a day. It has an unbearable allure that I just can't resist. And it's the only thing that cuts through the fog. It reminds me of everything I have ahead of me, and it reminds me that dreaming about it isn't enough.

Stupid, brainless, blind duck, I think. Haven't you ever heard that every newspaper has a masthead? And do you not know what all's on the masthead?

The address, among other things.

I get out of the tram at the next stop and hop on the other one—the one going in the opposite direction. I go as far as the main train station. I buy a ticket at one of the machines there and settle into a seat on the stinking commuter rail line to Frankfurt.

It'll have to work without a map.

It works fine. At the main station in Frankfurt there's a map on the wall. I find the right street. My name's not Maria and I can read a map, no problem. It's just three measly stops away on the subway.

I end up in front of a building that is not at all as imposing as I had imagined it would be.

It's a gray box, taller than it is wide. Above the entrance is the name of the paper in blue lettering. I step through the glass door and come to a sort of counter. Behind it sits a pretty young woman who smiles at me. Next to her is another woman, a bit older; she's on the phone but she smiles in my direction, too.

Something like shyness stirs inside me.

"Good afternoon," says the woman not on the phone. "Can I help you?"

I clear my throat and forget for a second why I'm there. The woman smiles patiently. Her gaze keeps wandering to the rolled up copy of the paper I'm holding in my sweaty hand.

So this is what it looks like, I think. This is where it happens. I feel awestruck.

"Do you have a question?" The woman won't let up. Her smile doesn't fade one bit.

I force myself to come back and engage, rather than float away as I've been doing for the last few days.

"I'd like to speak to someone," I say, and flinch because it sounds surprisingly loud.

"Someone in particular?"

"Yes. Susanne Mahler."

"Do you have an appointment?"

"No," I say, and gulp.

"One moment, please." The woman drops her eyes and reaches for the phone. She presses it to her left ear—which has a little pearl earring in it—and looks at me again. She asks something, but I'm distracted again.

"What?" I ask like Anton. And then correct myself the way I correct him: "I'm sorry?"

"Your name, please."

"Sascha. Sascha Naimann. Tell her that it's . . . Vadim E.'s stepdaughter."

"Vadim E.? Sascha Naimann? OK."

She dials a number and starts to talk. I watch her lips move and I rock my dangling sneakers back and forth like a pendulum.

The woman on the phone raises her voice and looks at me. "Vadim E., you said? Sascha Naimann?"

"Yes."

She listens to the person on the other end for a moment and then hangs up.

I look around for security officers, expecting to be escorted out.

It's probably stupid, but I feel as if I'm standing in a temple I'm planning to desecrate.

The woman speaks to me again, but I miss the first part.

"Ms. Mahler will be down to get you in a moment."

"To get me?" I'm briefly startled. The receptionist can't do anything about my associations.

"Yes. She said she was coming right down. Otherwise I would take you to the reception area—but there's no need."

"Reception area?" I ask like an idiot. But just then a door opens off to the side and I see them. There are two.

I know which one is Susanne Mahler right away since the other one is a man. I look at his face as he approaches. He's a tall man—his face is well above mine. He's not old, but his hair is completely gray. He's in jeans and a white shirt and a dark blue sports coat.

I hate men, I think absentmindedly. Do I hate men?

He extends his hand. "Ms. Naimann?"

I nod and at some point it occurs to me that I might shake his hand. I wipe my moist right hand on my jeans and briefly grasp his hand. Whatever name he says as we shake hands I miss. Then I shake hands with Susanne Mahler. Her hand is cool and soft, as if she's just put on hand lotion.

"This is Ms. Mahler," the man says.

"I figured," I say hoarsely.

Ms. Mahler is the same size as me. She's in her late twenties, maybe early thirties. She has short black hair playfully curled, red lips, and slightly squinty eyes. She's in a tight cream-colored top and dark pants. She has a very pretty face, but it looks less attractive the longer you look at it. Down to her waist she looks flawless; below that she's a little broader than she should be.

I look her in the eyes and recognize fear. She squints even more and lifts her chin to try to hide it.

I wonder why she's worried, I think silently. What could possibly happen to her in life? Then it hits me like a locomotive. She thinks I've come to register a complaint. I get it. I show up out of the blue, looking all aggressive.

And she is absolutely right.

Ms. Mahler and the man take me into an elevator. I remain silent, even though it's probably impolite. Ms. Mahler tries to smile at me. I try to concentrate and don't look at her. Better to look at the man, who is studying the numbers on the elevator buttons.

It seems as if he already knows what kind of mood I'm in, I think. If this silence keeps up, I'm not going to be able to concentrate. I've got to say something to him and Ms. Mahler. If I can't manage this, how will I ever kill Vadim?

They lead me into a square room with a big window. In the middle of the room is a round table. On it are a carafe, three cups, bottles of mineral water, and glasses. And a plate of cookies.

The man grabs the back of a chair and pulls it back from the table.

He doesn't sit down. Instead, he motions for me to sit down and then walks around the table to sit opposite me.

Ms. Mahler pulls her own chair out. Her face betrays such

panic that I already feel sorry for her. I think that I might want to reformulate my speech.

"Please, Ms. Naimann," the man says once we're all seated. "What's on your mind?"

I've never been addressed as Ms. Naimann in my entire life. Until today. And now several times. Every time I hear it I'm tempted to turn around to check whether there's someone else—Ms. Naimann—standing behind me.

They look at me attentively. Ms. Mahler fidgets a little in her chair.

I pull my newspaper out of my backpack and open it. Vadim's face lies in front of me and I put my fist on it.

"This is why I'm here," I say. "I read this."

"You are here about Ms. Mahler's article," the man perceptively summarizes.

I nod.

"What do you think of it?" he asks.

"It's shit," I say.

Ms. Mahler tries to smile but can't. I turn to her.

"Please excuse me," I say. "I don't mean to attack you personally, but it's hard not to when we're talking about something you wrote. I'm sure you're a good journalist. It's just that this article is . . . it's just not possible. You can't talk about him like he's a human being. You can't just write it that way. He shot my mother and another good human being. Just like that. That was his way of dealing with the fact that these people just wanted to lead a life without him being involved. If you did research—if you read the transcripts of the trial—you would know exactly what happened. He is the meanest, dirtiest, most disgusting scum that you will probably ever encounter. And you write that his letter is emotionally powerful. Or his sketches. Did you ever stop to think what reading that would do to me?"

Ms. Mahler opens her lipstick-painted mouth and says

something about a hundred thousand readers. She stops mid-sentence. I'm looking at her and can't see what caused her to clam up. It's possible a glance from the man that silenced her. The connection between those two pairs of eyes looks as tense as a piano wire. Or razor wire.

I'm glad I'm not directly between the two of them.

"I'm not sure how I should say this," I say. "I probably can't articulate all of this very well. But if Adolf Hitler were still alive, would you go visit him and praise his sketches?"

I know I've failed miserably and drop my head.

"I . . . ," Ms. Mahler begins to say and then stops again.

"Ms. Naimann," the man says quietly. I look up, surprised, and look him directly in the eyes. They are gray like the fog I'm hopelessly stumbling around in. "Ms. Naimann, I think I will be equally unable to articulate what is moving me at the moment. It's said that words are nothing but smoke and mirrors. It's a banal cliché, but unfortunately it's also true for the most part. I just want you to know that I thoroughly understand your feelings."

"If there's one thing I will never believe," I say just as quietly, "it's that you have even the slightest hint of an idea about my feelings."

Ms. Mahler lets out a horrified "Oh." The rounded mouth suits her. I look quickly at her and away again. The man nods.

"There's not much I can say in response to that. Any attempt to try to demonstrate my understanding is doomed to failure. Even if I were to use the word 'tragedy,' it seems to me it would probably sound like an arrogant attempt to encapsulate your fate in a conveniently empty phrase that could never possibly express the full extent of your situation."

"You are absolutely right about that," I say.

"But there is one thing I have to say," he says, and he sounds helpless and forlorn. Ms. Mahler shifts her gaze from me to him.

He turns to her and nods. I watch, astonished, as she stands up, politely pushes her chair in, offers me a pained smile and "goodbye and best wishes," and leaves the room.

"Actually," I say amid the silence, "I wanted to talk to her."

The man leans back and puts his hands on the table. "What would you have said to her?"

"That her article was shameless and stupid."

"You already made that clear. And besides," he says, pausing to push the plate of cookies toward me, "besides, she already knows that."

"What? I'm sorry?"

"She knows because I already told her."

I look at the cookies. There are square and round ones with chocolate icing, shortbread, star-shaped cookies with a dollop of jam in the middle, and some that look like spirals.

"Please help yourself," says the man. "Would you like something to drink? Coffee? Mineral water? We have cola in the canteen—I can go get one for you."

I shake my head.

"I want to tell you something, something I would otherwise never tell an outsider," he says, taking a round cookie. "Then perhaps you will understand a little better why Ms. Mahler isn't here for our conversation. Perhaps you will also not find the article so . . . outrageous. Ms. Mahler is an intern. She is working here as part of a work experience program. And—just between you and me—she's not one of the best of our interns. Not even a decent one."

I look at him. He has taken a bite of his cookie and is turning what's left around in his fingers.

"I was out of the office when her piece was published," he says. "Ms. Mahler wrote it up quickly after her thrilling visit to the prison, there was space open on the page, and so it appeared the next day. There it was in the paper. For your information, we have a policy whereby anything written by an intern must be read by an editor and, if necessary, rewritten. Within our strict standards for what we consider worthy of publication, there is some room for discretion. It can depend on the individual taste of the editor, on time pressures, or on any number of other factors. I must admit the person responsible for editing this piece did not exercise due diligence. To call what this piece needed 'editing' is itself a euphemism. Because the problems in Ms. Mahler's piece are not limited to a few stylistic mistakes. If you are going to take on this subject, it can't be done the way she did it. It should have been approached completely differently. And I'm afraid Ms. Mahler was not the right person for the assignment. Her reporting was completely unacceptable. For you, someone affected by the events, it was even less acceptable. There's no way else to say it."

I listen silently as if hypnotized by the rotating motion of the half-eaten cookie.

"I find myself having to take responsibility for something that cannot be justified. Whatever you criticize us about, you will be completely in the right."

"Why do you have to?" I ask.

"I'm sorry?"

"Why do you have to take responsibility?"

"Because I'm the section editor," says the man flatly. "I am in charge of the local news. When I came back from vacation, I gave Ms. Mahler and my co-worker who ran the piece an earful. That's why she was a bit nervous when you honored us with your unannounced visit. I had told Ms. Mahler that, as a result of her little ditty, for the first time in my career I hoped our paper wasn't being read and that the family of the victims never came across it. My wish was not answered. I ask for your forgiveness from the bottom of my heart."

He sticks the rest of the cookie in his mouth and smiles at me. It's a crooked smile because his left cheek is bulging out.

"I'm so sorry," he says suddenly with his mouth full. "I followed the news about the case two years ago. And not just for professional reasons. It created a sense of shock and dismay in me that exceeded anything I had experienced in the course of my work in years. I'm very sorry."

I nod.

Then we're both silent for a while. I listen as he chews up the cookie and swallows it. Then he pours himself a cup of coffee and reaches for the cream.

"What can I do for you, Sascha?" he says as he does. "You can dismiss that as an empty offer, but I would actually be willing to do a lot to try to ease things for you. Do you have any ideas about how I could do that?"

I try to think. Not that I expect to come up with something, but I want to be able to answer in a way that doesn't sound stupid for once. My best moments so far have been silent ones.

A white rectangle with letters on it pops into my field of vision. I put out my hand. The rectangle is put into the palm of my hand.

You are capable of reading, Ms. Naimann, I think to myself. You taught yourself how to read when you were four. And ever since you've read everything you could get your hands on.

So read it.

I read: Volker Trebur, Editor, City Section. There's an address, telephone number, email, private address, and phone number.

I look at him quizzically.

"Call me when you think of something I can do," he says. "Hang on, my mobile number's not on there." He pulls a pen out of his chest pocket, takes the white rectangle from my hand, writes a row of numbers on it, and puts the card back in my hand. "It would be an honor," he says flatly.

I try to shove the business card into my pants pocket. But when I stand up to do that, I drop it on the floor. I bend over to pick it up and crumple it in my fist.

"Is it a deal?"

"What? I'm sorry?"

"You'll come up with something?"

"I don't know if I'll think of anything," I mumble. "I'm not very creative."

"I don't believe that."

"Then don't." I pull my backpack onto my shoulders. The man stands up quickly.

"Thanks for letting me in," I say. "It's nice to be taken seriously. I'm off."

"I'll take you down," he says and opens the door for me. We ride the elevator silently. The card wriggles in my hand like a captured butterfly. Maybe it just feels that way because my hand is shaking.

At the glass door I turn to him. I'm expecting to have to shake hands goodbye. I don't like shaking hands and don't think I'll ever get used to it.

But he doesn't try to shake my hand. He puts his hand on my shoulder and says "Good day."

"Good day," I answer like an echo.

I take the subway, the commuter rail line, and the tram. The business card in my hand has stopped wriggling. I open the apartment door with the other hand and toss my backpack in the corner beneath the jackets.

That's when I see them—the shoes.

I wouldn't have noticed them if I hadn't tripped over them. They're big, stained leather shoes. The laces hang limply from them.

Huh, I think lethargically, and shove them aside with my foot. I want to go straight to my room. But I stop at the door to my room and turn around to look back at the shoes again.

It's a riddle, I think. A pear, a banana, an apple, and a circular saw: which one of these things is not like the rest?

It's nice operating in a gray fog, I think to myself. Gray is a nice color. It's underrated. Ignored. Has a bad reputation. But I'm warming up to it.

"Maria," I call out, surprising even myself, "there are some shoes out here."

The answer comes quickly, high-pitched, kind of surprised. It's not a word so much as an "Oh!"

"What is that supposed to mean?" I say angrily.

Maria appears in the kitchen doorway. She's in flesh-colored tights and a floral-pattern blouse. She's frantically patting down her hair.

"Little Sascha," she says, her eyes wide. "You're home so early today. We . . . I hadn't expected you."

"What do you mean early?" I say. "I'm not early."

"You always have your get-together Friday afternoons," Maria says.

"My club," I correct her, realizing she's right. Fridays the philosophy club meets after school. I'd forgotten. "And so what? Aren't I allowed to come home when I want?"

"Yes, yes," Maria says quickly. "Of course, of course."

She looks a little pale to me today.

The circular saw is the correct answer. It is the only one of the four things that doesn't rot.

Instead of going into my room, I go to the kitchen. Maria blocks my path. I have to shout at her for a second before she steps aside. I take a step forward and make the big discovery.

Sitting at our kitchen table is Grigorij, the father of Anna's friend Angela. I recognize him from seeing him around. We always say hi to each other. He's short and wiry, has a black moustache and a messy head of salt-and-pepper-colored hair. He's in an undershirt and sweatpants, trying to hide behind his teacup. But he can't, even though it's a big cup. Steam rises from the cup. Grigorij's holding onto a spoon, the other end of which is in a jar of jam. The still life is completed by a plate of cookies.

"Hi, Uncle Grischa," I say out of habit.

Grigorij puts the spoon in his mouth and licks it off—probably just a displacement activity as he ponders his next move.

"Hello, Sascha," he says. I hear an unfamiliar rustle. I frown, concentrating, until I realize it's the sound of Grigorij's feet—in blue socks—fidgeting around beneath the table. Probably looking for his shoes.

"Your shoes are in the entryway," I say coolly. "Or do you already have a pair of slippers you keep here? Just don't tell me you use mine. I wouldn't know, because before today our paths haven't crossed in this house, have they?"

"You've got it all wrong, Sascha," he says. This gets me briefly fired up, because there's nothing I hate more than people talking ridiculous bullshit.

"What exactly have I got wrong?" I ask. Maria disappears like a shadow at noon and reappears just as quickly with Grigorij's shoes in her hand. She lays them deferentially at his feet.

"You might as well put them on for him, too," I say, looking at the wall. "Why half-ass it?"

Grigorij slips out of his chair and squats to tie his shoes.

"It's not right, acting this way, Sascha," he says, lifting his wrinkled face toward me.

"What's not right?" I ask loudly. It comes out that way because my anger is being tempered by a gnawing, sudden sense of pity. Just what I need, I think. *Her* genes. At exactly the wrong moment.

Couldn't I have gotten her beautiful eyes instead? Please?

Grigorij stands up. Even upright he's half a head shorter than I am. He still has to raise his head to look at me. And he does.

"What?" I ask. "What did I say? How's Angela? I haven't seen her in a while."

"Angela's not doing too well," Grigorij says. "She had her wisdom teeth removed, but they did a crappy job. Her whole face has been swollen for a week now. She can only eat through a straw. Her only consolation is that she's lost a bit of weight because she can't really eat. She's been jealous of all the skinny girls for years—especially you."

I grunt.

"I make her banana milk," Grigorij says, looking up at me from below. "With an electric mixer. It's cold and nutritious, and she can drink it. She complains, though—she's had it with milk. But I can't just wave a magic wand and make the swelling go away."

"It sounds awful," I say. "I hadn't heard."

Grigorij shrugs his shoulders and shuffles toward the door. Maria follows him to the entryway. They don't say a word to each other. Maria keeps her eyes fixed on his slumped back. She closes the door behind him. Maybe they had a chance to exchange glances as she did.

Then she walks past me back into the kitchen. I stand in the hall for a while and then go into the kitchen.

Maria's sitting at the table stirring the jam with a spoon.

"How come you didn't say goodbye to each other properly?" I snap. Though given the situation it's not what I really want to know. "Is that how they do it in your generation? No goodbye kisses and not so much as a see-you-later?"

Maria doesn't answer.

"How long has it been going on?" I ask.

She looks up at me. Her little blue eyes are welling up.

"Don't cry," I warn. "And where are my siblings?"

"Alissa is at Katja's," Maria answers immediately.

"Who is that?"

"A friend of hers. Lives on the third floor. They play together a lot."

"I had no idea they played with each other a lot these days."

"And Anton has soccer practice at school."

I look at her.

"Sascha," she says, "I look after those kids as if they were my own. In fact, I consider them my own."

"But they're not," I say curtly.

"I've never once left them unattended. They are always my first priority. I would never do anything to harm them."

"You send them away and fuck around!" I scream. "Thank god I didn't get home any earlier. If I had caught you in the act—if I'd seen that old wrinkle bag with not just his shoes off but his ugly-assed pants off, too, I would have puked."

"It's not right, acting this way," Maria says glumly. It occurs to me that I've already heard this sentence once in here today. I turn around and go into my room. I throw myself on the bed and press my face into the pillow. I feel sick.

The door I just slammed closed begins to quietly open.

"Get out," I shout.

"Sascha," Maria says quietly, "what have I done wrong?"

I sit up. Maria comes in slowly, gingerly, as if she's entering a lion's den. Then she sits on the corner of the bed, close enough that I can smell her perfume. It makes me feel even sicker.

"He so nice, Sascha. He's a good man."

"I don't want to hear that," I say. "I don't care."

"It's not as if it's just . . . it's not just about . . . the bedroom," Maria says, blushing. "But you're a big girl. So I can say that's not totally unimportant."

"Maria," I say wearily, "get out of my room. Spare me the details. I have a weak stomach."

"Do you know what it's like to be alone?" she asks.

I stare at her. "Who is alone?"

"Me," Maria says, surprised—as if I've asked her something so obvious. "I love living here with you and taking care of the place, and I love the children. But I'm a grown woman, Sascha."

All of a sudden I remember she's not 50, she's 37.

"Et tu, Brute," I say bitterly. "What is it you all find so great about it? Why can't you live your lives in peace, without wrinkly old cocks . . . anyway, you know what I mean. I trusted you. I thought we were your family."

"You are," says Maria.

"I should have known," I say. "You didn't come here for us. You wanted to find a man here, a better one than you could find in Novosibirsk. And all you managed to find was Grigorij. What now? Are you going to marry him and move out? Or is he going to move in here? Or will he just stop by for a quick fuck now and then and make you wash his laundry?"

"That's awful," Maria says. "It's just awful, what you're saying."

"The truth is always ugly," I say. "Around here they say the truth hurts worse than a punch in the face." She'll never figure out that I just made this up.

"Listen to me, Sascha," she says, trying desperately to lock eyes with me. "Grigorij is a nice man. He can't do anything about the fact that he's been a widower for so long. And he doesn't have it easy with that fat brat of his. He washes his own laundry, by the way—and even irons Angela's skirts. And he's always been so helpful when I run into him on the street or at the supermarket. He's explained so much to me."

"What didn't I explain to you?"

"And now for three months he's been coming here. I never go to his place. I don't like his daughter and she likes me even less. And anyway, I prefer to be here. I feel safer than I would someplace else. I've also told him he can only come when the little ones aren't here. And he's sticking to that. I call him when I can. I have so much time."

"That's the least you can do—make sure the kids aren't around for it," I say and am horrified to see Maria's crying. "What's the problem?" I say with malice. "What grounds could *you* possibly have to cry?"

Maria shakes her head and wipes her tears away with the

sleeve of her shirt. Then she pulls out a big, floral-pattern handkerchief from the waistband of her tights and blows her nose. It sounds like a clap of thunder.

"I'm so lonely here," she sniffles into her handkerchief. "I never thought it would be so awful here. I don't understand anything here. Not even the TV shows. And the Russians here in the neighborhood all look at me funny. Grigorij's the only one who is always nice to me."

"Why does everyone look at you funny?" I ask, surprised. "Half the people around here are from Kazakhstan or wherever. Haven't you been able to make any friends?"

Maria shakes her head like a wet horse. "I think it might have something to do with the whole history."

"What history?"

"They all know I'm related to *him*. And, you know, when something like that happens to a family they are shunned. It's like a disease, and nobody wants to get infected. It was like that even in Novosibirsk."

"I don't give a shit what happened in Novosibirsk," I say and drop myself down onto my pillows.

"Don't be mad at me, Sascha. You have your hell and I have mine," Maria says. Then, with surprising grandiosity, she adds: "It's my burden and I'm going to bear it. I am not the type of person who would abandon children."

After she leaves I hear her call from the hallway: "Grigorij is a real sweetheart."

It sucks that you can't suffocate yourself with your own pillow, I think to myself. Could I ask Maria to help me?

I lie there for a long time with the covers pulled up over my head. I can see Grigorij's face in my mind, but it begins to blur and is replaced with Vadim's. Now there's a new one, I think. Jesus, girls, can't you get by without it? Why can't you be self-sufficient? Why do you want to be groped by someone like Grigorij or Vadim? Is there a gene for masochism on the X chromosome?

I hear the doorbell ring and Anton's bright voice breaks the silence of the apartment. Half an hour later Alissa's squeals join in.

I pull the covers down off my head and look at the telephone on my desk.

I've been thinking about it for an hour already and keep chasing the thought from my head. I don't know why I'm even thinking about it. I try to tell myself it's because of Grigorij. I just can't accept his presence. Maybe it's good for Maria and not bad for Anton and Alissa. But I can't stand it.

I smooth out the business card on my knee and dial the handwritten number. The last thing I feel like is talking to a secretary.

I let it ring for a while. I'm about to hang up. If voicemail kicks in I'll listen to his greeting and try again later. If I don't lose my nerve in the meantime.

And then he picks up. He says the two syllables of his last name in one breath, as if he's just run to pick up the phone.

"Good evening," I say as a wave of shyness suddenly washes over me.

"Yes?"

"It's Sascha Naimann," I say. Now I've done it. I can't hang up now without losing face.

There's a long pause. I scrape my fingernails across the face of the business card and silently hurl insults at myself. Before I'm finished cursing myself out the voice is there again, louder and more calm.

"Sascha? What a surprise. Now I can talk."

I've forgotten what I want to say.

"Is everything okay?" he asks in a friendly tone. "Are you still there?"

"Yes," I say. "It's about your offer."

"My what?"

"You said I could call you if I had a problem."

"Ah, yes, of course," he says. "What's the trouble?"

"I can't stay here at home," I say authoritatively.

"Why not?" he says, shocked.

"Just the way it is," I say.

"Got it. And what can I do?"

I take a deep breath. "I need a place to stay," I say. "I need to get out of here—at least for a few days."

He is silent for a while. I count off the seconds: five, ten, fifteen—at seventeen he speaks.

"Have you thought," he says, "about a hotel?"

"Whatever," I say, closing my eyes and uttering a silent, incoherent prayer—despite the fact that I'm not religious.

"Or were you thinking . . . I don't mean to be too forward, I'm just trying to understand what you mean . . . Would you like to stay over at my place?"

I open my eyes and swallow the gasp that wells up inside me. "I don't know what your situation is," I say. "Tell me if it's a stupid idea. I don't care where I go, as long as I don't have to sleep here."

"We have a guest room," he says. The "we" stabs painfully at my ear. "I just want to be sure I haven't misunderstood you. If you are looking for a place to stay and you're asking me for help, it goes without saying that I'm willing to put you up—but there are other places, as well."

"If you don't have anything against it, I would opt for the former arrangement," I say. Suddenly I don't care anymore. "Where do you live, by the way?"

"In Bad Soden," he says. "Not right in the town center—in a section a little ways out. But I can't pick you up until five-thirty. I'll wrap up a bit early. Does that work?"

I can't believe my ears. "You're going to pick me up?" I ask, feeling that for the first time in two years fortune is smiling on me. "Here at home, is that what you mean?"

"You haven't moved, have you? If you use public transport

it would probably take you two hours. I'll pick you up at five-thirty."

"Great," I say. I've gotten up now and I'm dancing in place in my little room. I feel like jumping and singing.

"I'll just need your address."

"My what? Oh, of course." I tell him the address and mix up the street number and the apartment number. It takes a few attempts at straightening it out before he finally reads back the correct address.

"Perfect," he says patiently. "Just one more thing. Call me if you change your mind, okay? Call my mobile. You have the number."

"I'm not going to change my mind," I say. "You can call me if you change yours."

"Right, see you in a bit," he says calmly and hangs up.

I open my wardrobe and throw some underwear, jeans, and a hoodie onto my bed. I shove it all into my backpack. I grab a toothbrush from the bathroom and return to my room, spinning around looking for things I might absolutely need.

But I don't need anything. Shortly after five I go into the kitchen. It's filled with the smell of crepes. Maria, keeping watch over a cast iron skillet, steps out of the plume of smoke. Alissa is standing on a footstool staring at the skillet as intently as if a cartoon were being shown in it. Anton is sitting quietly at the kitchen table drawing. I look over his shoulder—it's a row of black tanks in flames.

"Maria," I say, "ever heard of a ventilation fan?"

"What?" She turns around and ducks her head down.

"Alissa," I say, "it's time you took care of these things. There's a switch up there—Maria should turn it on before she starts cooking. That way the whole apartment won't stink of fish or cauliflower or burnt crepes. We won't see each other for a few days. I'm going to a girlfriend of mine's place."

Maria would never dare to ask questions. But Alissa has no such inhibitions.

"Which friend?" she asks, turning her jam-smeared face to me. "Do you have any girlfriends?"

"Yes," I tell her. "She lives in town. I'm going to stay with her for a few days. It's totally normal."

"When are you coming back?" Anton asks.

"We'll see," I say. "I'm taking my mobile. Call me if anything comes up."

"Good," says Alissa. Maria remains silent.

"The crepes are burning, Maria," I say. She turns around, grabs the skillet, and flicks it. The crepe flies up, turns in the air, and lands back in the pan.

Maria has a lot of these artistic moves up her sleeve.

"Take me to the door, okay?" I say to Maria. "Be good, you little hooligans. I'll see you soon."

"See ya," Anton says, and Alissa waves with a wooden spatula. Maria follows me to the apartment door and stares at the backpack in the entryway. Her lips tremble.

"Did you say something?" I ask her.

"Is it . . . " she says, barely audible. "Is it because of me and Grigorij? For god's sake, sweetie, I never thought that this would be such . . . please, Sascha, don't do this to me!"

"Don't be so dramatic, Maria," I say firmly. "Everything's fine. I'm just going to see a friend. I'm old enough. Take care of the little ones. Don't let them watch too much TV, read to them, make sure they do their homework—even if you don't understand it. And make sure they eat some fruit."

"I buy fresh fruit every second day," Maria starts to say, but I silence her with a wave of the hand.

"Call me if anything comes up."

She looks at me sadly.

"I think it's good that Grigorij only comes over when the kids aren't home, got it?"

She nods so forcefully that her double chin wobbles.

"Then everything's all set. See you soon." I throw my backpack over my shoulders.

"Little Sascha," Maria says, "Not that I care one way or the other, but do you really have a girlfriend?"

I look at her blankly.

"The thought had crossed my mind," she says, coming closer so she can look me in the eyes. "You've got something against men. Maybe it's better for you to be with women. The most important thing is to have someone."

"What?" I scream. "It's not that type of girlfriend. I'm not a lesbian. Unfortunately. But I'm not one."

"Then maybe . . . " Maria's face takes on an impish look, "Maybe it's actually a boyfriend?"

I think for a second and then nod.

"You caught me," I say. "It's a boyfriend. See you later."

I head down the stairs.

At quarter to six, a silver Audi winds its way into the complex. I'm sitting on a planter, trying to calm my racing heartbeat. I hop down once I can see the license plate.

He gets out and waits as I walk over.

"Hello," I say, smiling like an idiot.

"Good evening. You still want to get out of here?"

"Otherwise I would have called you back."

"Good." He opens the trunk. "Give me your bag."

I hand him my backpack. He holds it up as if he's gauging the weight.

"Is that it?"

"Yeah."

"Okay." He opens the passenger door for me. It smells nice in the car, new leather and decent cologne.

He gets in. "Last chance to hop out," he says seriously.

I hold tight to the sides of the seat.

He notices, smiles, and turns the key in the ignition. "Off we go," he says.

We're silent for almost the entire trip. I have to keep myself from looking over at him too often. I look straight ahead as houses, trees, and street lamps rush past. The car glides quietly and easily over the asphalt, but I continue to hold onto the sides of the seat as if I might fall out.

Once we're on the autobahn he glances briefly in my direction.

"Put your seatbelt on," he says.

"Huh?"

"Please put on your seatbelt."

I grab the belt and wrestle with it for a while before I finally manage to click it into place. He turns on the radio for the six o'clock news. I peek at him sideways. He's concentrating on the road ahead, his hands on the steering wheel. He has big hands and not a single ring on his fingers.

I feel butterflies in my stomach.

"Do you know where Bad Soden is?" he asks without looking at me.

"Not really," I say. "Somewhere around here."

"True."

Two miles of stop-and-go traffic, the radio says. It's music to my ears. I'm hoping we make no progress at all.

I lean back and feel the cool leather on my back. All of a sudden I'm incredibly tired. I'm interested in who is waiting for him—and for me—at his house. But not that interested. I'll find out soon enough.

"Look," he says. "Frankfurt."

I look out at the concrete desert off to the right of the highway with its silhouetted skyscrapers. "I know," I say. "Nice."

"What's nice?"

"Frankfurt. I like big cities. They look best when they are lit up at night. I've liked that since I was a kid."

Then we are silent again.

I close my eyes and try not to smile. Then I jump, startled by a shrill, grating noise.

"The windshield wipers," he says as I relax back into the seat. "It's raining."

"But the sun is shining."

"And it's raining."

The wipers smear the dusty drops across the windshield. Gleaming holes have been punched through the gray clouds exposing patches of improbably blue sky.

"Do you think there'll be a rainbow?" he asks.

"No," I say. "It would be too kitschy."

"Life is kitschy," he says. "Nothing but kitsch and clichés and things you've heard a hundred times before, tasteless plot-lines and dialogue that wouldn't make the cut in any halfway decent screenplay. A rainbow over the Frankfurt skyline—what would you think of that?"

"It's just blind rain," I say.

"Sorry?"

"Blind rain. Haven't you ever heard that before?"

"No."

"That's what you call it when it rains while the sun is shining."

"That's what who calls it?"

"People where I live. Have you really never heard of it?"

"No, never. We don't call it that."

Soon he exits the autobahn. The car zips around through an area that's more rural than I expected it to be. In one field are sheep—hard to believe they stay outdoors overnight. He looks over at me. One corner of his mouth turns down. "Not the big city here," he says.

"So I see."

Around another bend and then we go steeply uphill. He stops at the top of the slope and puts on the emergency brake.

"We're here," he says. "Welcome."

I open the passenger door.

It's a big house next to a few others along the ridgeline. He holds open the gate for me and we go up some stairs to the door of the house. There are flowers to the left and right of the door and lawns beyond.

"It's beautiful," I say unprompted.

The entryway is dark and cool. I start to take off my sneakers.

"You can leave them on," he says. "The floor's cold."

"I'd rather not," I say. I'm standing in my socks in front of a big entryway mirror, trying not to look at myself in it.

He has my backpack slung over his shoulder.

Now what, I think.

And for a moment I'm happy not to have any parents to be accountable to. I feel free. There's not a single person who cares whether I misbehave here. I can do whatever I want. I'm in charge of myself.

But I'm still nervous.

The house is very, very quiet.

"Are you tired?" he asks. "Do you go to bed early? Normally?"

"Depends," I say. "If I have to get up early, then yes. But lately I've slept through entire days."

Weighty conversation here.

"I'll show you the guest room," he says. "Come on."

He walks ahead and I follow. There are a lot of stairs in this house. At one stage I hear a noise I can't place. Screechy, fast, but off a ways.

"What's that?" I ask, but so softly he doesn't hear me.

"Have a look," he says. "This look okay for you?"

He opens the door to a room that's twice the size of mine at home. My room at home is only eighty square feet. Here there's a bed at the window, and the light-colored sheets seem to glow in the dark room. Next to that is a heavy old bureau, a little round table, and a rattan chair.

I take a step and am inside the room. I breathe in the air,

the scent of freshly washed linens. I take another step and am face to face with a glass door that leads out into the garden.

"What kind of tree is that?" I ask. "The one with the white blossoms."

"Cherry," he says. "Can you not tell? Behind it are blackberry patches. But they won't be ripe until August."

"I don't know anything about trees," I say. "My mother knew a lot. She always explained what you called various herbs and all that, but I never cared. I have a hard time remembering things that bore me."

The silence he answers with is awkward.

"Thanks," I say sheepishly. "For the room. It's really nice here."

"My pleasure," he says. "Are you hungry?"

"No," I say.

"What do you mean? What do you like to eat for dinner?"

I think. He does, too.

"We have bread and cheese in the house, I think," he says. "But I can also order a pizza."

"I'm fine," I say. "I'm going to go to bed."

"You should eat something. You are already so thin."

"I'm just kind of tired."

"Okay. There are towels in the armoire. The bathroom is over there. You need anything else?"

"A book," I say. "I didn't bring anything to read."

"What do you like to read?"

"Doesn't matter," I say. "Everything."

"Then you can pick something out yourself. Come on, I'll show you the living room—that's where we keep the books."

We.

"I'd rather you recommend something."

"Okay."

I sit down on the bed. He puts the backpack down at my feet and looks at me.

"Would you like to have some time to yourself?"

I nod.

"Call me if you need anything. I'll be . . . somewhere in the house. I'll pick out a book for you."

"Okay."

He closes the door. I hear his shoes squeak on the wood floor.

I take off my socks. Who else lives here? Do you have a wife? They would have been such easy questions. Curiosity is not a sin but it can get messy. That's what my mother always said. It's a Russian expression, too. She was very curious. I'm not. Maybe that's why I experience things early. Usually earlier than I would like.

I pull my pajamas out of my backpack. I open the drawer of the armoire and touch the snow-white bath towels perfectly folded inside. I pull one out. In the process I step on my mobile—it must have fallen out of my backpack.

I pick up my phone and hold it in my hands until it's warm. Then I dial the number.

"We can't pick up the phone right now!" screams Alissa's voice in my ear.

"You should answer 'Alissa Naimann.'"

"I know!" she shouts. "Sascha! When are you coming home?"

"Soon. But not yet. Why aren't you in bed?"

"We're reading."

"What are you reading?"

"Little Red Riding Hood."

"Do you like it?"

"Nope. Little Red Riding Hood is stupid. She should be able to tell it's a wolf and not her grandmother."

"Maybe she doesn't want to see. Maybe she is so afraid of the wolf that she wants the wolf to think she believes him. She's fooling herself, thinking he won't hurt her if she plays along."

"It's baby stuff."

"No, no, it's actually quite grown-up. Say hello to the others, Alissa. Tell them I called. Sleep well."

Alissa hangs up without saying goodbye. She probably nodded her head. She doesn't understand that people can't pick that up over the phone. She holds pictures up to the phone. Once she even held up a piece of cake. "Smell that," she said. "Fresh out of the oven."

I walk down the hall to the bathroom. It's gigantic, gleaming, covered in mirrors. I feel like the hooker in the movie "Pretty Woman." It's an unsettling feeling. I lock the door, throw my clothes onto the bathmat, and get into the shower. I stand under the piping hot water for half an hour—until my skin is all red. Afterwards I wrap myself in a towel and comb my hair.

With my clothes in my arms, I walk back toward my room in my pajamas. I hear the strange noise again. It also sounds as if people are talking upstairs. Quiet, distant voices, but I can't tell whether it's two or more.

I'm relieved when I make it into my room and close the door.

There's a pile of books on the bureau. I look through them: the autobiography of Marcel Reich-Ranicki, John Irving's latest novel, Max Frisch's *Homo Faber*, and *Der Schwarm* by Frank Schaetzing. Next to the books are two apples.

There's a bottle of mineral water and a glass on the round table now, too.

I look around more closely. I even kneel down and look under the bed, to see if anything has wriggled its way under there. I'm not sure what I'm looking for—or perhaps I don't want to admit what it is to myself.

But there's nothing else to find. So I lie down in bed, stick my mobile phone under my pillow, pull the covers over my head, and close my eyes. I don't cry.

I fall asleep quickly. When I wake up again it's dark outside. I grab my mobile and look to see what time it is. Three-thirty in the morning.

I sit up.

I know exactly where I am. But suddenly I'm frightened and uneasy—much more so than earlier. The blossoming cherry tree in the garden spreads its ghostly boughs across the window.

I'm cold. My hair is still not completely dry.

Maybe they have a hair dryer in the bathroom. Of course they do.

I push aside the covers and put my jean jacket over my pajamas.

I can't find my socks in the dark—or the light switch. I tiptoe into the hallway.

Right now I wish from the bottom of my heart that I were home. It's so intense my eyes almost well up with tears. Maybe next time you should think of that before you do something like this. Thinking first is probably a good idea in general.

Upstairs must be the bedroom where the owner sleeps. Or owners? I heard multiple voices. Or were they just voices coming from a TV?

I turn the corner and find myself in the living room. I have to shield my eyes because there's a bright TV on. The sound is off. Christina Aguilera is dancing on the screen, her blond dreads flying around and her mouth straining. She seems distraught that she's unable to make a sound.

Against the wall is a couch, long and oddly shaped, like a giant shrimp. There's a mound on the couch.

Shit, I think, trying to back out of the room.

But the mound begins to rise. It sheds its husk—a blanket. I retreat, startled, and step on the remote. Christina Aguilera's voice blasts through the air at full volume.

The noise is so jarring that I squat down and put my hands over my ears. My eardrums feel like they've just burst. And it's still loud as hell. The mound on the couch morphs into a human shape, jumps onto the floor, and pounds a button on the remote.

The TV screen goes dark. I can hardly believe how immediate the silence is. I stand up again. In the dark, I can't tell who is standing in front of me.

But one thing is clear: It's not a woman.

"You can stop covering your ears. I turned it off."

"What?" I ask.

The person in front of me grabs my wrists and pulls my hands away from my ears.

"Hello," I say, pulling my wrists out of his hands.

"Hello."

He takes a step back and sits back down on the couch. Throws the blanket over his legs and looks me up and down. It's a guy, skinny, but tall—must have been a head taller than me when he was standing. I have no idea how old he is. His hair falls to his shoulders in scraggy strands.

"You must be the . . . ," he says, knitting his brows.

"Sascha."

"Right. Volker told me about you. You stayed out of sight all evening. I was wondering where you were hiding."

"I was tired. I fell asleep."

"Aha."

I lean against the wall and examine him. He's still eyeballing me unapologetically.

"I'm Felix," he says. "Can you understand me?"

"Can you understand me?"

"Don't be insulted. Volker said you were Russian."

"Yeah, so?"

"Why are you so pissed off?"

"I'm not pissed off."

"You speak good German."

"Thanks. You, too."

"I fell asleep out here, too," he says. I can see his teeth in the dark as he smiles. "I was lying awake for ages. So I came out to watch TV and fell asleep at some stage. Until you decided you needed to wake me up by cranking the speaker up full blast."

"You were already awake. You sat up—that's what startled me."

"True, I was half awake. But I only really woke up after that jolt."

I smile despite myself.

"My name is Felix," he says.

"You said that already. I'm not that forgetful."

"Seriously? I am."

"I think I heard you earlier," I say. "Voices upstairs. Was that you?"

"I only have one voice. But it could only have been me or Volker. Or the computer or the TV."

"Only you or Volker?" I ask.

He looks at me quizzically.

"Yes," he says. "Nobody else lives here. Other than a few friendly ghosts. Haven't you seen any of them? There's a swarm of them under the bed in the guest room."

I smile back at him.

"Do you know *Calvin and Hobbes*?" he asks.

"No."

"It's a comic strip. Calvin's a little boy and Hobbes is his stuffed animal—a tiger. In one strip Calvin is sitting on his bed, scared, and asks, 'Are there ghosts under the bed?' And from under the bed comes a speech bubble saying, 'No.' Then Calvin, trembling, asks, 'If there were ghosts under my bed, would they be big or small?' And the speech bubble from under the bed says, 'Very small.'"

"Hmm," I say. "Funny."

"You want to see my room?" Felix asks after a pause.

"Why?" I ask.

"Why not? Volker said you'd be staying a few days. Said you had your reasons. But he didn't say what they were."

"I'm sure he had his reasons."

"How old are you?" he asks distrustfully.

"Seventeen."

His face relaxes.

"I'm sixteen," he says. "I thought you were more like fifteen."

"Tough to tell in the dark."

"True. You could be in your late twenties."

"Yeah, thanks a lot."

"No, I mean, it really is tough to tell. Lots of girls look older than they are and lots of adult women look young."

I shrug my shoulders. I'm not interested in discussing this topic. But Felix apparently is.

"Recently Volker brought one home," he says, "who looked to me like she was in her early twenties. But she was thirty-six! Somebody from the office. Susanne."

"Mahler?" I ask meekly.

"Do you know her?" he asks, elated. "How? Do you have something to do with the paper?"

"No, not really," I say. "Is she here a lot?"

"Susanne? Twice. About three months ago. Then never again. Why do you ask—is she married or something?"

"No idea," I say wearily. "I don't give a shit about Susanne."

"Got it," he says. "I don't either. Do you want to see my room now?" he asks again. It seems childish to me.

But I like children.

"Fine by me," I say.

As we walk down the hall, his size strikes me again. He's wearing a crumpled T-shirt and baggy dark pants.

"Do you guys have electric lighting?" I ask.

"Why do you ask?"

"Because we seem to be constantly in the dark."

"It's nice."

"I don't think so."

"Really?" He starts to feel around on the wall.

I wave my hand. "Forget it. It can't be too many more miles to your room, right?"

"Nope. It's walking distance." He stretches his arm out and opens a door right in front of me.

"Here's where I live," he says. "Have a look."

I'm impressed and stand there taking it in.

It is a gigantic room—at least five times as big as my room at home. The bed is a wide, low space piled high with blankets and pillows. On his desk is a computer. There are two keyboards in front of the computer, and two video game consoles. The stereo display blinks. There's a TV hanging above the bed—right now it's showing news.

"Not bad," I say. "But all these electronics—don't they give off radiation?"

"What do you mean?"

"Electromagnetic radiation. Isn't it supposed to be bad for you?"

"I'm unhealthy enough already," he says, laughing. "A bit of radiation isn't going to kill me."

"And such a massive bed—you could play soccer on it."

"Yeah—and other games." He grins at me.

I turn away.

"I'm going back to my room," I say and then correct myself. "To the guest room."

"Yeah?" he says, disappointed. "And then what?"

"Then I'll go to sleep," I say, even though I think I'll go read.

"Hmm," he says. "Should I show you the way?"

"Thanks, but I'll find it, I think." Now that I know I'm not going to bump into a woman in a negligee, I feel much more at ease. It occurs to me that maybe I don't only hate men. Maybe I hate women, too.

I can't get up the courage to ask him where the other bedroom is.

"Is Volker your father?" I ask timidly.

"What did you think?"

"I didn't think anything. Goodnight."

"Sleep well," he says. I have the impression he's following me with his eyes as I walk out.

I wander around the house a little. The wood floors creak underfoot. Here and there a carpet muffles the sound of my footsteps. The place smells like dust and vanilla.

I think I've figured out which door is his. Just a feeling. I stand in front of it and try to think. Then I realize how stupid I'd look if the door opened and I was standing there. So I go back downstairs quickly and quietly and slip into my bed. I look at my phone. No calls and no text messages.

I fall asleep with a half-eaten apple in my hand.

In the morning, sun pours through the slits of the blinds.

I know this feeling from when I was five years old and stayed with my grandmother—pure, unadulterated joy, when everything you sense hints at even more happiness. The clatter of dishes, the light, the buzz of bees, voices in the kitchen, the scent of fresh-brewed coffee and warm cinnamon on the rolls my grandmother had just taken out of the oven.

I lie there for a long time taking it all in. It's different from that time, but somehow very similar. I look at my phone. It's just after ten.

I get dressed and comb my hair. It's finally dry. There's a mirror on the wall above the armoire. I look warily at myself in it. I don't look anything like my mother. Even ignoring the difference in hair color, she was stronger looking and had different facial features. Everything about her was different. Not even my eye color is right. And my eyes are small, and I squint a lot because I'm a little shortsighted—and when I get upset.

I toss my hairbrush into my backpack.

It doesn't take me long to find the kitchen. I had stumbled upon it last night. It's one of those kitchens that opens onto the living room. There's a guy sitting at the table with a T-shirt on that reads "Apocalyptica" on the back. I have a hard time squaring him with the guy I met last night. I have to think for a moment before his name comes back to me. Felix. Latin for "happy."

I'm surprised to see that in the light he has strawberry blond hair and freckles. With the sun on it, it looks like his hair is on fire.

I stare at him in wonder for a few seconds. Then he flinches and starts to turn around toward me.

"Good morning," I say. I clear my throat and try again. "Good morning."

"Hello," he answers quickly.

Something about him is different from last night. He looks at me for a second and turns back away from me. He seems tense.

"Have a seat," it occurs to him to say. "What would you like to eat?"

"I don't care."

"Well, there's the butter and jam, there's the cheese, and here's the milk. Do you drink coffee?"

"Yes."

"And here's the orange juice."

"Thanks." I sit down. He passes everything to me—the basket of bread, the plates, a knife, the coffee pot, a cup—until the area in front of me is totally packed. I take my elbows off the table.

"Thanks," I repeat.

"We also have Nutella."

"I don't eat it. Thanks."

"You don't eat Nutella?" Now he sounds a little bit like he did last night. "How is that possible?"

"I'm not big on sweets."

"You're lucky."

"Why?"

"I can eat half a jar of Nutella in one sitting."

"Go ahead then. What's so bad about that? I've heard alcoholics don't like to eat sweets. And the other way around—that people with a sweet-tooth have a lower risk of becoming boozers. So be happy."

He looks surprised. "Where did you hear that?"

"I can't remember. Read it somewhere."

As I'm spreading butter on a piece of bread, I notice him stealthily trying to check me out. I look up and he glances away.

"Where is . . . "

"Volker?" volunteers Felix.

"Yeah."

"He has a meeting this morning. Said I should look after you."

"And you are."

"Yep." He stares at the tabletop.

Then I get it.

"Felix," I say, "what did your father tell you about me?"

He looks away. Bingo.

"Go ahead," I insist. "I'm not going to flip out. I won't even get a bit upset."

He remains silent.

"Come on, Felix. Did he tell you about . . . about my mother?"

Felix nods and looks over at me. "Why are you laughing?" he says, appalled.

"I always laugh when I shouldn't," I say. "Let me guess what he told you. He said that my mother was shot by my stepfather. That it created quite a furor. A huge story that made headlines all across the country. That I'm a poor little orphan—but a smart one, and one whose story is well known. And that you shouldn't bother me with questions. Am I right?"

Felix goes so pale that his freckles stand out. "That's not the way he said it," he mumbles hoarsely. "It was that you . . . that your . . . that . . . there was a family tragedy or something. What you said . . . is that . . . is that all true?"

I sigh. "Where was the cheese again?" I ask. "I'm not into jam."

Felix jumps up and nearly knocks his chair over.

"Here," he says, still looking at me in shock. "I . . . uh . . . I don't know what to say."

"It's the same for most everybody," I say. "You're in good company." I smile encouragingly at him. He grimaces back.

"Hey," I say. "Life is beautiful. Sometimes. You know who you look like?"

"Yeah, I know," he murmurs. "The guy who plays Ron Weasley in the Harry Potter movies."

"Yes, but more in the later movies. When he had long hair."

"Have you seen them?"

"Yeah," I say seriously. "Because of my mother. She loved Harry Potter. Like loads of people. She couldn't wait for each new installment. And then . . . you know . . . I had to watch the last movie . . . without her."

I stand up and walk to the window.

When I turn around, big Felix looks very small sitting in his chair. He looks at me fearfully. I sit back down. Felix fidgets in his seat like Anton.

I try to imagine what Anton is doing right now.

"I have to make a quick call," Felix says, getting up.

I nod, lost in my thoughts, trying to picture the scene at home.

A few minutes later I grab the John Irving book out of the guest room, lean it up against the juice bottle and read while finishing my breakfast.

That's how Volker Trebur finds me.

He really scares me. I don't hear him come in. He's carrying a big box of groceries, puts them down on the table with a sigh, and bends to see what book I'm reading.

I jump.

"Did I startle you?" he says, smiling. "Enviable concentration power."

"Hello. No, not startled."

"Good morning. Did you sleep well?"

"Yes, very well."

He sits down opposite me and shakes his hands. "Heavy box," he says. "I'm Volker."

"Sascha." I close the book, suddenly thinking it's rude to have it open with him there. I start to load the dishes into the dishwasher.

"Sascha," he repeats pensively. "I don't want to pry, but what was wrong at home?"

"What do you mean?"

"You needed to get away so badly. Does that happen a lot?"

I gather the dirty forks and knives. I try to shrug my shoulders.

"There was unpleasantness," I finally say, but it doesn't sound very convincing.

"Are you eighteen already?"

"Almost. Seventeen and two months."

"Does your guardian know where you are staying?"

"My guardian," I say, "doesn't know a thing, unfortunately. Not a thing. I can go where I want. I said I was going to a friend's place. They can reach me on my mobile if there's a problem at home."

"So," says Volker, reaching out and breaking off a piece of a croissant that's in the bread basket, "you think it's all right for you to be here?"

"I don't think it," I say. "I know it. Family services are never going to try to charge you with kidnapping."

"Uh-huh. Very comforting."

"I can leave if you don't want me here."

"That's ridiculous." And then, after a pause: "You've already met Felix."

"Yes. Last night."

"Yes, I heard. Thank goodness I sleep with earplugs in. Though I think I still felt the vibration."

"What vibration?"

"From the TV when you stepped on the remote."

"Oh, yeah, that," I say. What did I think he meant?

"Monday is a holiday," says Volker Trebur.

"Yeah?" I say indifferently. "Which one is it now?"

"May Day—first of May."

"Aha."

"But Tuesday you have to be back at school."

"Let me worry about that."

"Are you going to skip?"

"I don't know yet."

"Do you want to get a doctor's note?"

I sigh.

His eyes are laughing. "Am I getting on your nerves?" he asks.

"No," I say and lose myself in his gaze. "But I must be getting on yours."

"Not in the slightest," he says seriously. "And I think Felix is pleased."

"Not anymore," I say. "I gave him the whole tragic family history over breakfast. He's still in shock."

Volker Trebur's face tightens. "He didn't . . . "

"He didn't ask a thing, no. I told him on my own. I just assumed he already knew."

"Yeah," Volker says slowly, "it's hard for him to deal with things like that."

"He'll manage," I say a bit bitterly. "After all, I managed."

"Please excuse me," he says. "For god's sake, I'm sorry."

"No problem."

I pick up the book again. I'm not sure what to do. Stay here or go back to bed or out into the garden? The magic of the morning has dissipated. Not sure when or why.

"I knew your mother," Volker says as I'm deciding what to do.

"How?" I look at him.

"I was introduced to her once. She received an award, for . . . " He squints and snaps his fingers. "It was an oddly phrased citation. Something like 'aiding successful integration.' I was on the jury. Sometimes you get asked to do these types of things."

"Poor you."

"Yeah, you're right. I shouldn't complain. Anyway, that was the setting."

"So you saw her in passing? Or did you hand her the envelope with the 300 euros in it?"

"Why so prickly? I talked with her. She was an extraordinary woman."

"Did you notice that right away?" I ask excitedly.

"Yes," he says calmly. "I did."

I fidget with the pages of the book.

"That's why I was so shocked to hear that she . . . " He hesitates and cracks his knuckles. A horrible noise.

" . . . was gunned down," I say. "Shot in the head, in the stomach, in the . . . "

His face changes.

" . . . in the legs," I continue. "Luckily in that order. I think as a result she didn't feel much. Why are you so pale?"

His hands fall from the table to his lap and his fingers interlock.

"Oops," I say. "Have I said something you didn't already know?"

"Stop," he says, not meeting my gaze. "Please stop."

"Does it sound grisly? I thought you would have seen all the articles, because of your job. Every entry wound was thoroughly discussed in the press. Have to keep people up to speed."

"Not those details," he says barely audibly. "I haven't read about those."

"When it's about someone you know a little, it all sounds very different, right?"

"Stop," he says, suddenly getting up. "Please."

"Volker," I say slowly. "Did you possibly know my mother a little better than that?"

He sits down heavily and folds his hands. "What do you mean by that?" he asks.

"It's crazy," I say, "how small the world is."

"What are you talking about?" he asks haltingly.

"Why don't you want to admit it?"

"I don't have anything to admit, Sascha," he says and looks at me. His gray eyes are dim.

"Are you embarrassed? Was she not good enough for you? Or did she reject you? I can't imagine that."

"Sascha," he says loudly, making me flinch, "what do you want from me?"

"What I want—from you?" I ask pensively back at him. He sits at the table with his shoulders slouched, rubbing the bridge of his nose between his eyes with his thumbs. He looks exhausted.

I'm beginning to feel sorry for him.

"I'm sorry," I say. "It's none of my business. And it's ungrateful of me to give you such a hard time when you've been so hospitable to me and put me up here."

"No, that's nothing," he says, pausing. "I just don't want you to get the wrong idea about me."

"Keep it a secret," I say and look out the window at the cherry tree. "Come on, there's no point in making our lives any more difficult. It seems to be a painful topic for both of us."

In the afternoon he leaves again. He says he has a meeting. I hope it's not that he can't stand to stay in the house with me because he's afraid of all my questions.

I would like to run my fingers through his hair. I'm curious whether it's soft like Anton's or wiry like mine.

I go out in the garden and lie on the grass, looking up at the clouds. Felix comes out.

"Oh, you're here, too," I say, surprised.

"And so are you," he says.

"You stay home a lot?"

"Always," he says. "I wanted to ask if you wanted to watch a DVD with me."

"What movie?"

"I've got hundreds. Some new ones, too."

I pull myself up and brush the grass off my jeans.

Inside I stand in front of his DVD collection for a long time. The same news channel from earlier is on the TV.

"I don't like action films," I say. "Or love stories. Or horror movies."

Felix groans. "Is there anything you do like?"

"In theory, yes," I say, continuing to look through the DVDs.

"Do you want to watch my favorite movie?" he asks, blushing a little.

I'm expecting it to be a James Bond movie or "Mission Impossible." But Felix surprises me. "The Cider House Rules," he says with a bit of embarrassment.

"The John Irving book," I say with surprise. "He wrote the screenplay, too, right?"

"I don't know," he says, looking at me quizzically. "You want to watch it? It's such a good movie." He beams when I nod yes.

He rips open a bag of chips and starts the DVD. I sit Indian style on his bed. He stretches out beside me. At one stage his knee touches me briefly and he pulls it back as if he's gotten an electric shock. I want to tell him I don't bite, but I refrain from saying anything.

"It's a bit sad," he says five minutes in. "I don't know if you . . . if it's something you . . . "

"Jesus," I say, "I'm not going to cry on your shoulder because of a movie. I've only ever cried from a movie once."

"Yeah?" he says. There's curiosity in his voice but his eyes never leave the TV screen. "Which one?"

"Have you ever seen 'My Girl,' with Macaulay Culkin? He dies after getting stung by bees—he's allergic to them. And at his funeral, his little girlfriend—whose father runs the funeral home—completely breaks down. She starts screaming that she has to give him back his glasses, that he can't see without them. And he's lying there dead. And she's screaming, 'He needs his glasses!' I always get choked up and cry during that scene."

"Oh," he says, glancing sideways at me for a second. "Was it always like that or only since . . . ," he trailed off.

"This was before my mother died," I say. "It's an old movie."

"Oh," Felix says again, grabbing the bag of chips.

After that we don't talk anymore until the credits have rolled.

"Do you do that, too?" he says as he's putting the DVD back in its case.

"What?"

"Watch the credits. Until the very end."

"Yeah," I say, surprised. "Always have."

"Me, too," says Felix. "At the theater, too. It bugs me when people jump up and leave as soon as the last scene is over. I always want to see who made the music and all that. So many people work on a movie—you have to give them their due by at least reading their names."

"I haven't been to the movies in ages," I say. "It's been years."

"Did you notice anything about that movie?" Felix asks, blushing again.

"Like what?"

"The girl in the orphanage—the one who falls in love with Homer."

"What about her?"

"She looks a little like you."

"What?" I cry. "That weird chick?"

"She's not weird," he says indignantly. "She's really pretty. She just has a weird role. And she plays it really well."

I raise my eyebrows.

"You want to see?" Felix asks. He jumps off the bed and goes over to his computer. He hits a key. The screen lights up immediately—it was just sleeping, not off. I stand next to him and watch him open and close tabs.

"What am I . . . ," I start to say, then see it—a website called Paz-de-la-Huerta.

"What's that?" I say. "What is Paz de la Huerta?"

"It's the girl. The woman—she's 22 now."

"What's her first name?"

"Paz."

"And why are you showing this to me?"

"So you can see. See that you look alike."

He clicks on a photo gallery. I lean closer. He pushes the chair to me and kneels on the floor.

"See?" he says. "Am I right?"

I click through the gallery. It's mostly stills from the movie we just watched. The dark-haired girl from various angles. Fifty-two shots.

"Well," I say, "I guess she really isn't that awful-looking. Especially when she smiles."

"Told you," he says. "Like you."

"What?"

"Nothing."

"Unbelievable," I say. "Who would go to so much trouble to build a site for such a minor actress? Somebody would have to be crazy—and have a crush on her. And have nothing better to do."

Felix bites his lip.

"I run this site," he says.

"You?"

"Yep, me. It's my website."

I can't think of anything to say.

"There's also a guy in Hong Kong," Felix says. "He helped me a little. But he doesn't take it as seriously as I do."

I don't know what to say. I certainly can't say what I'm thinking. Felix would be insulted.

"You spend a lot of time on your computer," I finally say.

"Yeah," Felix says equally flatly. "A lot. Almost all my time, really. Either that or I watch DVDs."

"How come you don't go out?" I ask. "I'm sure there are girls out there for you—better ones than Paz."

Felix doesn't answer. He pulls the keyboard over toward himself.

"I mean, I don't care one way or the other," I say. "But isn't it a little lonely?"

"So?"

"I don't think it's good when people just waste their lives away," I say with a harshness that surprises me. Felix isn't listening, though. He's typing.

I see the words he's typing as they appear on the screen.

*And you? Are you living your life?*

He shoves the keyboard over to me. I think for a second and type: *My situation is different.* Then I write in capital letters, *TOTALLY DIFFERENT. Don't even think about comparing yourself to me.*

*I'm not*, Felix types quickly. I reach to take the keyboard back but he holds onto it. A new sentence pops up on the screen.

*Do you have a boyfriend?* I read. Then he hands me the keyboard.

*No*, I type. *I don't want a boyfriend.* Then, thinking of Maria, I add, *Or a girlfriend.*

*Have you ever had one?* Felix writes.

*What?*

*A boyfriend.*

*I got "married" at camp once, when I was 14. Just for a laugh. But I haven't had one for the last two years.*

*Because of your mother?*

*My mother had nothing to do with it.*

*I would love to meet somebody like Paz. Even better would be Paz herself.*

*Good luck.*

*Who would you like to meet?*

*Nobody*, I write. But that's not entirely honest. But I don't want to tell him I want to run my fingers through his father's hair.

*Maybe somebody older*, I write instead. I hand the keyboard back to Felix. He lets his mouth hang open.

*Have you ever . . . ?* he types.

*What?*

*You know.*

*Fucked?*

He goes completely red. Even his ears flush. He types three letters: *yes*.

*I already told you. No.*

*What? You're 17 and you haven't yet?*

*So what? You haven't either.*

*Don't you think it's weird?*

*I'm a fundamentally weird person.*

*But haven't you ever wanted to see what it's like?*

I have to laugh. *With you?* I add a smiley face at the end.

Felix thinks for a while. Then he types two words: *Why not?*

I snort with laughter. But I don't dare look at him. I can almost physically sense his awkwardness.

*I'm not Paz,* I write. *Even if I do have brown hair.*

*That's got nothing to do with it,* Felix writes. I look over at him for a second. He's staring at the monitor.

*You're pretty,* he writes.

"What?" I cry out. "Are you crazy?"

He doesn't look at me. He winces. I don't say anything more.

Talking is against the rules.

I think for a long time. I think about Volker Trebur. Half of Felix's genes are from him. But you can't see it in him.

*Did your father used to have red hair too?* I write.

Felix reads it over a few times, as if he can't understand the question.

*Yes,* he writes finally. *Why?*

*Let's do it.*

*What???* He writes. His fingers hang in the air expectantly. I take the keyboard from him.

*What you wanted to do. Just don't grunt too much.*

*What do you mean?* He's flushed to the base of his neck. I'm unaffected. *I'll try my best,* he types, quickly adding, *Try not to grunt. Not sure if I'll be able to.*

Then we just sit there for at least five minutes, not looking at each other.

Felix speaks first.

"I think you're scared," he says, his fingers gripping the edge of the table.

"What about you? Are you scared?"

"No way."

"Then take off your clothes."

He turns slowly to me. He couldn't get any brighter red. You could light a match on his forehead.

"You first," he says.

"As if. It was your idea."

He looks at me. His face is tense. Then he strips off his T-shirt and throws it on the floor.

"Your turn," he says, wrapping his arms around himself like he's cold. There's a long white line running down the center of his chest. It stretches to below his breastbone. His arms can't cover it.

"What's that?" I ask, pointing. "Is it a scar?"

"It's nothing. It's your turn. I've already taken off half my clothes."

"It doesn't count the same," I say, buying time.

"Why not? I don't know why people get so worked up about nakedness. Every woman has all the same parts as other women. Every man has all the same parts as other men."

I take a deep breath and add my sweater to his T-shirt on the floor.

"That, too," he says, pointing with a nod of his chin.

"Oh, that which we dare not name," I say.

"What?"

"Nothing. It's Goethe," I lie and throw my bra in his face. He grins as he catches it.

"Why are you staring at me like that?" I say coldly, restraining myself from wrapping my arms around myself like him.

"I guess not all women look the same after all," he says.

I stretch out my arms, still sitting on the chair. He kneels in front of me so I can put my hands on his shoulders. His fingers carefully touch my ribs. His face is too close. I shut my eyes and manage to kiss him on the mouth. Probably because he leans in toward me.

Then I make two surprising discoveries. First, the hair the sunlight is on—that is, on the back of his head—is soft and very warm. Second, he has firm, dry lips that feel nice.

I lean back and look into his wide open eyes.

"Stop staring at me," I say, pulling him closer between my knees.

Later, we're lying next to each other between two comforters and at least five pillows. The bed is really just a wide mattress sitting on the floor, I think. I listen as a buzzing mosquito keeps desperately slamming itself against the windowpane.

Felix gulps. "So?" he asks, after he stops coughing.

"So what?"

"So what was it like for you?"

"Sticky," I say. "And you?"

"Intense," he says, relaxed. He adds with pride: "I didn't grunt at all."

"I noticed."

"But I almost exploded as a result."

"Fortunately only almost."

"No, actually I did."

I have to laugh.

"Did it hurt?" Felix asks.

"Is it supposed to? No, it didn't."

"Me either," he says.

The mosquito stops buzzing. I savor the silence. The only problem is that Felix is taken over by a sudden spell of talkativeness. He turns onto his side and snuggles up to me.

"If it wasn't that great for you," he says in my ear, "it's just because you're inexperienced and need to practice more."

"What?" I shout. "You're the one who needs to practice."

"Okay," he says quickly, "let's practice some more."

"Not with me."

"Then with who?"

"Try Paz."

He pulls himself a few inches away from me. "You're really mean," he says, hurt.

"I know. And you're really chatty. I thought men fell asleep right afterwards?"

Felix curls up. "Not me," he says. "I don't feel like sleeping. Not at all."

"Then give me my clothes. They're over there on the floor. With yours."

"Why me? Why don't you get them yourself?"

"Because you are the man here."

This seems to make him brighten. "You can't look," he says sternly. I pull the covers over my face.

"Where is your mother anyway?" I ask from under the covers.

"Here," Felix says. "Hey, you're not supposed to look!"

"Yeah, but when you say 'here' what do you expect?" I say.

"I meant there."

I look where he's pointing. The TV that's been going the whole time. A man and a woman are anchoring a news broadcast.

"What do you mean, there?" I ask.

"The woman on TV—that's my mother."

"No way," I say. To say I'm surprised is an understatement.

"Why not? That's her."

Just then their names appear in subtitles beneath their faces. Johann Keller and Martina Trebur.

"Amazing," I say. "What's she doing on the tube?"

"That's her job. You can see that. In Berlin."

"Are your parents split up?"

"Yeah, of course."

"Why did you stay with your father?"

"Why wouldn't I? I didn't want to move to Berlin. And I don't like her new boyfriend. I like it here. I have everything I need right here." He throws me my sweater, pants, and socks one after the other. He turns off the TV.

"Should we go out somewhere together?" says Volker that evening.

"Where," says Felix suspiciously.

"I was thinking we could go someplace for dinner. Maybe that Italian place you liked recently, Felix. No reason always to stay home. Or we could go to the movies. What do you think, Sascha?"

"I don't know," I say. "Whatever."

"You say that about everything. What a couple of drips you both are. I was different at your age."

"What were you like?" asks Felix and closes his eyes, relaxed.

"I definitely didn't waste my weekends sitting around at home."

"Home," says Felix, "is the best place."

"I should take away your computer."

"Over my dead body."

"If you want to go out, I'll go with you," I say. "To the Italian place, to the movies, or both."

"Well, if you two are going, I'll go," says Felix. "I'm home alone all the time."

"My point exactly," Volker says.

We get into the silver Audi and drive to a neighboring town where there's a little cinema. Felix and I sit in the back seat because we can't agree on who should sit up front next to Volker. My gaze jumps back and forth between the back of Volker's gray head of hair and the view out the window. Felix looks at me. I don't look in his direction because whenever I do he looks away sheepishly. So sheepishly that it's as if this afternoon never happened. As if we just met.

I find it funny.

Before we go to the movies, we sit at a dark wooden table at the little pizzeria. Volker orders wine. "I'll have the same," says Felix, and so do I. We trade toppings from our pizzas. I give Felix the cheese from mine; I take his mushrooms and hot peppers. We laugh a lot.

"Give me that," says Felix, reaching out with his fork.

"Hands off my plate," says Volker. "This is for me and me alone." He observes us with a sympathetic and somewhat wistful gaze. I feel suddenly sad. Felix tells a joke and I forget to laugh.

"What's showing?" I ask.

"At the cinema? 'Brokeback Mountain.' About gay cowboys. They finally got a copy of it here," says Volker. "Everybody else seems to have seen it twice already."

"There's no point to going to the movies," Felix says. "Not anymore. Cinemas are dying out. The movie will be out on DVD soon anyway."

"But I want to see it on the big screen," Volker says. "You're just not interested in the film because there aren't any girls in it."

"None at all?" asks Felix, appalled.

I sit between the two of them at the movie.

It's an old-fashioned cinema, everything covered in plush, dark-red velvet. Volker has put a huge bucket of popcorn on my lap. The place is full. My elbow rubs up against Volker and he doesn't pull his arm away. I break out in a sweat.

Felix keeps reaching into the bucket of popcorn.

"Just take it," I whisper.

"I don't want it," he whispers back. Then he forgets to take his hand out of the bucket and leaves it on top of mine. It's warm, moist, and covered with popcorn crumbs.

I carefully pull my hand away.

Felix pulls his out of the bucket.

Volker has in the meantime moved his arm. His eyes are fixed on the screen. I look at him in profile for a long time. Either he doesn't want to notice or he really doesn't notice.

I shake Felix's hand off my knee in annoyance and shake the bucket of popcorn off my lap in the process.

After half an hour I forget about everything else because the movie gets interesting.

Shortly before the end of the film, a woman in the row behind us starts to cry—so loudly that I'm distracted and turn around to look at her. Right then Volker and I exchange a glance. His lips open. He mouths a word. "Sad," I think he says, and I shrug my shoulders questioningly. He points at the seat next to me with his eyes.

I turn around and look at Felix. His face is all wet.

Volker's lips move again. "Console him," I hear.

"I don't want to," I whisper.

Felix looks over at us suspiciously and wipes his face with his hand.

Afterwards Volker waits patiently as we watch all the credits. We walk silently to the car. Felix's eyes are red. I know he's embarrassed about crying.

"What did you think?" Volker asks. There's no answer for a while.

"Good," I say finally, because I don't want to be rude. But I don't feel like talking about it. "It was pretty decent."

"What enjoyable company," Volker mumbles. "What lively conversation. Next time I'll take somebody from the nursing home. They couldn't be less lively than you two."

We drive home in silence.

I'm happy when I flop down on the white bed in the guestroom. It no longer smells so unfamiliar. It occurs to me that I haven't called home yet. They haven't called me either. I consider sending a message to Maria. One of those voice messages, where you type in a text message and a computer reads it aloud at the other end. Preferably something in Russian—it sounds particularly strange when the speech synthesis program tries to pronounce things written in a foreign language.

I try to think of something funny to write. But then my door opens slowly and quietly and suddenly Felix is standing next to my bed in a T-shirt and boxers.

"You?" I say in an unfriendly tone. "There's no way I'm going for it twice a day."

"I didn't come for that," Felix says quickly. "You said your feet get cold. Volker always turns the heat down overnight. He's always too warm."

"When did I say that?" I say, realizing in the same instant that my feet are indeed cold.

Felix sits down nervously on the edge of the bed. He has a questioning look on his face.

"Suit yourself," I say, moving sideways to make room for him to lie down next to me.

The bed is much narrower than his. The tips of our noses touch. I can feel his fresh breath. It smells like toothpaste but also, oddly enough, like chocolate. It's as if he has just eaten a chocolate-covered mint. In the dark his pupils are so dilated that it looks like he has black eyes.

I throw the covers over him and roll over so I'm not facing him.

He shifts around a little and then snuggles up to me. I'm warm immediately.

He wraps his arms around me and clasps his hands in my lap. I unclasp them and hold them so they don't start to wander around.

"They're good right there," I say.

"Here?"

"Yes."

"And what about here?"

"Not there."

Felix sighs in my ear.

"Do you want to sleep?" he asks.

"Yes."

He sighs again.

I lie there awake for a long time. Felix's breath stirs the back of my hair at regular intervals. I can feel the hair move back and forth.

I think about the cowboys in the movie and can't fall asleep.

"Felix," I say quietly, "do you want to hear a story?"

He jolts awake. I can hear him blinking.

"Don't know," he says. "Depends."

"It doesn't have a happy ending," I say.

Felix is silent, breathing.

"There was once a woman," I say. "A pretty woman, who was smart in her own way. But in other ways she was stupid. She couldn't protect herself. At some point she fell under a spell and was struck by a sort of mental blindness. She got married to a man and had two kids with him. She already had an older daughter from a previous relationship."

Felix holds my feet between his. It feels good.

"Her husband was a rotten man," I continue. "The woman kept wanting to leave him. But he always hemmed and hawed about how she couldn't leave him. She probably thought he'd have a complete breakdown at some point. Or perhaps she wanted to have a breakdown herself instead. The man was short-tempered and jealous, and he shouted at her a lot and sometimes hit her.

"One day the whole family moved to another kingdom. The spell was broken. She managed to kick the asshole out. He was absolutely irate, hit rock bottom, and so forth. But she left him anyway.

"He settled down a little. He regularly visited his old family, as he called them, especially his two sweet kids. He didn't get along well with the older daughter, who wasn't his. She had always hated him and he knew it. He was also afraid of her. He knew that if he so much as laid a hand on her, on either of his kids, or on the woman, the older daughter would go straight to the cops.

"One day the woman met a prince. But he was disguised and nobody realized he was a prince. She was happy for a while, and so were her children. He really was a prince. When he was around, everything was good.

"But the ex-husband wasn't happy about this. He saw how well his old family was doing without him. And he saw that his former children loved the prince, too. He was worried they would realize what an asshole their father really was. He wanted to stop this from happening. He wanted to do something about it and came up with a plan.

"He bought candy for the kids. He went to see his old family and none of them realized that on this day he had a pistol beneath his jacket. He gave the kids the chocolate. The woman was home, too. Along with her prince. And the man began to curse them out—until they asked him to leave.

"And he left. But he didn't go far. Instead he turned around. He rang the doorbell. The woman let him back in. The older daughter arrived home just then, too.

"'What do you want now?' she asked. 'Come back when you've calmed down.'

"That's when he lifted the pistol and fired it. Once, twice, three times, four.

"The older daughter began to scream. She screamed so loud that one of the windowpanes shattered. She tried to prop up her mother, but she weighed too much and was limp and lying in a pool of blood. Then the daughter jumped on the man with the pistol in his hand. She punched him and even managed to break his nose.

"She still doesn't know to this day why he didn't shoot her.

"He threw her to the floor and snarled, 'Where is he?' He meant the prince, who was sitting in the kitchen with the children. The prince came running out, shaking with fear and horror. The children came running, too, and saw their mother and began to scream. The man lifted the pistol again and the prince attempted to save himself, running into the bedroom. He closed the door behind him but the man shot through the door.

"The older daughter ran out of the apartment with the other two children and rang the neighbor's doorbell. From the hall they heard two more shots. The neighbor jerked the children inside and slammed the door shut again.

"Soon the man with the pistol came out of the apartment and also rang the neighbors' doorbell. But they wouldn't let him in. The man said to call the police. Which was exactly what they were already thinking.

"The man waited on the stairs until he was arrested. He gave up the pistol without any protest and confessed. In court he said his wife had annoyed him forever.

"Felix, are you asleep?"

I run my hand along the goosebumps on his forearms. He doesn't say a word. His breathing is silent. Maybe he's holding his breath.

"Were you even listening?"

"Where's your father?" he asks suddenly, startling me.

"Don't know. Maybe here somewhere."

"What do you mean?"

"I don't know anything about him. I don't want to know. My mother tried to talk about him a few times, but I always stopped her."

"I don't understand," he whispers in my ear.

"Little Felix," I say, "how could you possibly understand? He didn't want me to be born. That's the only thing my mother ever got out before I shut her up once and for all. He wanted my mother to have an abortion. And he gave her quite a bit of money so she could have it done privately at a doctor's office instead of at one of those clinics where women were practically put on an assembly line and not given any anesthesia. My mother always said he was a respectable man who was able to set up a respectable abortion for his girlfriend—she said that again and again, only half-joking. She went to the doctor's office and was told to undress. Then she thought—or at least she says she did—'But I want to have a little girl, and I want to call her Sascha, and I'm not going to end this life, this thing's alive no matter what this man says. I want to have it.' So she got dressed again, took the envelope of money back, and walked out. The doctor thought she'd gone crazy. My mother ran the whole way home because she thought the doctor would come after her. She never wanted to see the man who had impregnated her again because she was afraid he might try to induce an abortion by violent means. There had been a few recent cases like that. At first she was going to give him back the money, but then she bought baby things with it instead.

"That's why I don't want to know his name. He's not even on my birth certificate. There's nobody to ask, either, now that my mother is dead. He could have won the Nobel Prize for all I know.

"But I don't care. What do you think, Felix?"

He doesn't answer. He's very quiet. There's just a soft whistling sound in my ear. I'm not sure what it is. Could be from a mobile phone somewhere, I think.

Then I fall asleep.

I wake up in the middle of the night.

I can't understand what's happening. Felix is lying next to me on his back, trying to say something. He feels funny and looks strange. I hold his hand. It's cold and shaking.

"What is it?" I say. "What's wrong?"

He opens his mouth and wheezes.

I get nervous. "What's wrong?" I ask. "Say something!"

His hands fall to his chest and start to feel weakly around. His fingertips hop up and down on his T-shirt as if he's typing on an invisible keyboard. His lips move. I lean down to him and he breathes in my ear.

"Volker," he gasps. "Get Volker."

I sit up, jump over Felix onto the floor and run out into the hall. I race to the door I think is the one to Volker's room. I yank it open but there's no bed in the room, just a table and several armoires.

"Volker!" I cry. "Where are you? Volker!"

I run through the house, pulling open doors and yelling. It seems to go on forever. Behind all the doors is darkness and a musty smell. An ironing board falls out of one doorway and hits me hard on the head. I barely notice. I feel like I'm lost in a labyrinth. Everything starts to spin. I brace myself against a wall but it seems to recede from my hand.

"Volker, god damn it! Something's wrong with Felix. Where are you?"

I begin to weep loudly.

Volker appears at the end of the hall. He's barefoot. His upper body is naked. He's buttoning his pants. He runs by without looking at me.

"Not in there!" I yell. "He's in my room."

Volker stops, turns around, and bounds down the stairs. I follow him. He's faster than I am. I lurch down the stairs and nearly fall over.

In the guest room, he tries to sit Felix up. I turn on the light. Felix's face is white and his lips are blue. There's panic in his eyes. Volker braces him by his shoulders.

"Water," he yells over his shoulder. "Get some cold water."

I run to the kitchen and throw open the refrigerator door. I look for a glass, find one, and fill it with water. Half of it sloshes out as I run back. Felix tries to drink. His teeth clank against the rim of the glass.

"What else can I do?" I ask, agitated. "Where's the medicine?"

"Shit," Volker says. "We've got to get to the car."

"You want me to look for it in the car?"

"No. We need to get in the car. It's not stopping. We have to go to the hospital."

Felix is moving his lips and looking at me. I go closer and kneel next to him. I can barely hear what he says. "Come with us," he says. "Please."

I pull my jeans on. Volker throws on a shirt. Felix puts up his arm as Volker goes to hoist him.

"I want to get dressed," he says through his clenched teeth.

Volker rolls his eyes. "Stop screwing around," he says. But I run upstairs, jerk open a drawer in his room, and pull out a pair of jeans by the ankles.

In the car I sit in back next to Felix again. His arm is draped around me while Volker floors it.

We hurtle down the autobahn at 120 miles per hour.

I don't understand what's happening. I hold Felix's left hand and rub it, periodically slipping down to his wrist to feel his fluttering pulse. I press down on it, hoping to keep him from passing out. I'd love to use my other hand to cover my other ear so I wouldn't have to hear the whistling noises coming out of his mouth, each one sending a chill down my spine.

Felix begins to collapse onto me.

"Volker," I scream. "He's losing it."

Volker throws his mobile phone over his shoulder into my lap.

"Call them. The number's listed under *hospital.* Tell them we're on the way. Give them our name."

I flip open the phone. It's much more complicated than

mine, and it takes some work to find the phone book and the right entry. Eventually I find it, push call, and hold the phone up to my ear. The sound of the road flying by under the car is so loud that I'm afraid I won't be able to hear them answer.

Somebody picks up the line and I barely make out the words "pulmonary care." I stammer and then say Felix's first name. I blank on the last name.

"Trebur," says Volker from the front seat.

"Felix Trebur," I shout into the phone.

"Can't breathe again. We can't get it under control," Volker says.

I repeat it like an echo.

I can't understand what the voice at the other end of the line says. Then it's gone.

"Got cut off," I say, distraught. "Volker, I lost the guy on the phone. What should I do?"

"Nothing," Volker says as calmly as anyone could possibly do while shooting down the fast lane in the middle of the night with someone about to croak in the back seat. "Thanks."

"I didn't understand what he said to me!"

"It doesn't matter. They know we're on the way. They know us well."

I cradle Felix's head in my hand, trying to make him more comfortable.

We get off the autobahn. I don't notice where we are—I'm looking at Felix. As I look at his face in the pale light of the road lamps, I realize it has taken on a color I've never seen in any living person before. I'm sure he's dead. I put a finger on his lips and am amazed to feel warm breath on it.

A mechanical arm across the road goes up. Then everything speeds up. Felix is whisked out and disappears on a gurney. Volker hurries out and runs after it with his hand gripping my upper arm. I let myself be pulled along. My knees nearly buckle.

Then we're sitting on plastic chairs in a hallway. For ages. After the burst of activity, it feels like time is standing still now. The glaring fluorescent lights make Volker's skin look yellow. He sits there with his legs spread wide apart, his head leaning against the wall, and his eyes closed. The top two buttons of his shirt are open. He's a mess, and it doesn't suit him. I'm tempted to tell him—or just to straighten him up myself.

"Volker," I say after a long time, "what color is my face right now?"

He rubs his eyes before looking at me.

Green," he says and leans his head back again.

"Volker," I say, "where are we?"

"At the university medical center," he says with his eyes closed.

"Volker," I say, "why are we here?"

He lifts a hand, blindly finds my shoulder, and pats me on the back.

I get goose bumps along my shoulder blades.

"Volker," I say, "what's wrong with Felix?"

"It would be easier to tell you what's right with him," Volker says.

I'm not sure what to say to that.

"Felix was born with lungs that don't always work," he says. "For the first ten years of his life he spent one month out of every two in the hospital. Then he got a transplant."

"Oh my god," I say.

"If you two slept together, you must have heard it. When it's quiet, his breathing sounds like a soft whistle."

I remember the noise I was wondering about as I fell asleep.

"I thought the sound was from a mobile phone," I say, and have the impression my ears have suddenly swollen and gone beet red. I touch them. They're hot, but the same size as usual.

"At first I thought I'd never get used to it," Volker says. "But you can get used to anything."

"What do you mean?"

"The sound of his breathing. When we would go on vacation and stay in the same room, the noise used to drive me crazy. I started sleeping with earplugs. That's why it took so long for me to hear you tonight."

"I didn't think it was so bad," I say. "The whistling, I mean."

Everything around us is quiet. The only sound is of muffled footsteps somewhere in the distance, down some other hall or behind some set of doors.

"The white line," I say. "He has a white line on his chest."

"That's the scar from the operation," Volker says. "He's ashamed of it. It's the reason he never goes to the pool. He thinks everyone stares at it."

"That's ridiculous," I say. "You can barely see it."

"I tell him that all the time. But he never believes me."

"What a crock of shit," I say. Then I'm suddenly embarrassed. "I'm sorry."

Volker opens his eyes and looks at me questioningly.

"For what?"

"That we're here. I figured everything was perfect for you. I thought you guys were happy people with no problems."

Volker lets out a joyless chuckle.

"Such a long scar," I say.

"He was cut open," says Volker. "They sawed his breastbone in half. So they could get at his bronchial tubes. He was in intensive care for a long time afterwards. A little boy with a million tubes stuck in him. Sorry, I know that sounds maudlin—but you can hardly take it when it's your kid."

"Of course," I say. "How could anyone not be affected by that?" I think of Anton and suddenly feel cold.

"I had a problem with my gallbladder two years ago," says Volker. "Gallstones—totally routine. I had an operation at a hospital. Minimally invasive surgery. Absolutely nothing compared to a lung operation. But even so, when the anesthesia wore off, I was lying there, and, Christ, it hurt so bad. I was begging for painkillers at every chance. And I couldn't stop thinking about Felix the whole time. He hadn't cried at all through his entire ordeal. Can you imagine how much it must hurt to have your breastbone sawed open? To have parts of your lungs cut out? Can you imagine how every breath must hurt after that? He tried to take shallow breaths so he wouldn't scream."

He doesn't look at me. He stares straight ahead.

"He never complained," says Volker. "He's never had it easy, but he never whined about it. Before the operation, there were lots of things he couldn't do. Couldn't play sports, no horsing around. He was a really sick child. Afterward things got better. With the transplant he was able to live a normal life—at least compared to the way he'd been forced to live prior to it. He has to take a lot of medications—to keep his body from rejecting the transplant, to keep his blood from getting too viscous—and everything has to be constantly monitored. He jokes that this place is his second home."

"But why are we here right now?" I ask. "Was the transplant rejected?"

"God, no," says Volker. "What are you saying? No. But for the last couple years he's had these attacks where he can hardly breathe. Allergic reactions or something. Over and over—out of the blue. The bronchial tubes seize up. The nerves in charge of the tubes just go haywire."

"The nerves?" I ask.

He holds up his hands and spreads out his fingers. "See, these are the bronchial tubes. And this is where the pulmonary lobes would be. Here's where the transplant is grafted on. With exertion, your breathing rate increases. That's normal. But with Felix, everything seizes up. He can't get any air. His body's oxygen supply is reduced. Emergency. As just happened."

"What causes it?" I ask, feeling suddenly guilty.

"Nobody knows," says Volker. "It's erratic. Though usually at night. I really can't say what the source of the problem is. I can't figure out any pattern."

"And the doctors?" I ask. "Do they have any idea?"

"No, they don't know, either. Felix is a riddle." He smiles. "A medical mystery. There's probably not a single allergen he hasn't been tested for. The assumption is that it's some rare genetic defect. And by the way, these attacks sometimes go away on their own. There are a few tricks that can help sometimes, too—like cold water. But it doesn't always work, obviously."

"And what happens if they can't get it under control?" I ask, and put my hand to my mouth.

"Well," says Volker slowly, "that would be bad. Very bad."

"What are they doing all this time?" I ask, after taking my fingers out of my mouth.

"I'm not sure. They have drugs they use to try to get it under control. A series of steps. If the first one doesn't work, they try the next one. Twice they've had to hook him up to a respirator because they had to give him such large doses of muscle relaxants to open up his breathing passages. You know what relaxants are?"

"Yeah," I say. "Medicines that put your muscles to sleep—they can stop your own breathing."

"Right," says Volker. "That's what happened to him."

I feel sick. "What is taking them so long?" I ask.

Volker doesn't answer.

"Volker," I say. "I think it's my fault."

He turns to me with a look of shock on his face.

"Yeah," I say, "we probably shouldn't have done it."

"Done what?" asks Volker.

My face flushes. It feels like a dozen bees have just stung me.

"Oh, that," Volker says, scanning my burning face. "Are you trying to say you took my son's virginity tonight?"

"No," I say.

"No?" he says. "It certainly looked that way."

"Not tonight," I say. "This afternoon."

Volker laughs. Here in the empty hospital hallway, it sounds horribly out of place.

"That's what happens when you leave children unattended," he says.

"We're not children," I say.

"Don't worry," he says. "I don't think it had anything to do with that. This has happened before. Although," he glances sideways at me, "it's been a while since it was this bad."

"Maybe he needs to conserve his energy better," I say awkwardly.

Volker laughs again. "Poor Felix," he says. "I'll never be able to tell him what he should do. I've never had any success with that."

"Stop laughing," I say. "Please. It's creeping me out. It sounds freaky in here."

Volker shakes his head in disbelief. "Little Felix," he says. "Who would have thought."

I don't like his tone or the topic.

Just then a door opens. A short doctor with dark brown skin and short black hair waves Volker over.

I stay seated and feel my heart slowly sink.

Volker shakes me by the shoulder. "You still with me?" he asks. "You seem to have checked out there. We can see Felix."

"Is he . . . ?"

"He's okay for now. He has to stay under observation."

"He doesn't have anything with him."

"That's exactly what he's going to say to me. Come on, we'll say goodnight to him."

"Is it okay?" I ask timidly.

"I'm sure. Come on."

We go up one floor. Up here the walls are even whiter, and

the silence is even more pronounced. There's a long wall of doors. One is open and a nurse gestures for us to come.

"Just be quiet," she says.

We enter the room. I'm scared about what we're going to see.

There are two beds inside. There seems to be someone sleeping in the bed nearer to the window. There's a dark-haired head on the pillow. In the other bed sits Felix, glaring at Volker. I can't believe how alive he looks. He's not blue anymore. Only later do I notice the cable running from beneath his T-shirt to a frightening-looking machine next to the bed.

"I want to go home," he says.

"You're not a little kid anymore," Volker says.

"Why do I need to be here?" Felix hisses.

"They want to keep you under observation."

"They didn't do that last time."

"You didn't almost die on them last time," says Volker sharply.

Felix starts to open his mouth, then closes it.

He's sitting on top of the covers in the jeans I pulled out of his armoire and the T-shirt he was in when he fell asleep snuggled up to me. He looks as if he's ready to hop up and go. One hand is balled up in a fist. The pointer finger of his other hand is in some sort of sleeve that's connected to another machine.

"I'll come first thing in the morning," Volker says. "We. We'll come first thing in the morning."

"I don't have anything here. No toothbrush, no computer, no pajamas, nothing."

"I'll bring it all in the morning."

"I want it now."

"Abracadabra. Felix wants it right now. That's crap. It's not going to happen tonight."

"You can cut the lecture."

I start to leave. I feel out of place.

But as I start to move, Felix notices me. He looks at me. And there's great disappointment in his face.

"Sleep now," says Volker. "We're going home to sleep too. It'll do us all good."

Felix's eyelids close halfway, depressed. He keeps looking at me without saying anything. I can't tell what he's trying to tell me with his look. I hope he doesn't think I'm going to spend the night here.

Volker turns the door handle.

"Four o'clock," he says, yawning. "What a night. Get undressed and go to sleep. You're a big boy."

"Idiot," Felix mutters.

Then I get the impression Volker wants to leave before me so Felix has a chance to talk to me privately. But I don't feel like hearing whatever it is he wants to say.

"Sleep well," I say quickly. "See you tomorrow."

I duck under Volker's arm and out into the hallway.

He catches up to me in front of a glass door.

"Where are you going?" he says good-naturedly. "That's the wrong door."

I turn around and walk along next to him until we're outside.

In the parking lot, I greedily breathe the fresh night air.

"What a night," Volker says again. "Look. Stars."

"Yep," I say. "A lot of them."

The drive back home passes like a dream. The gentle sway of the car makes me drowsy.

Volker turns on some music. "Dido," he says. "You know her?"

"Yeah," I say.

"Great, huh?"

"It's all right," I say. "I'm not a huge fan."

Volker pushes the buttons on the CD changer. "Mary J. Blige?" he says. "You like her?"

"That's fine," I say. "There's worse."

"Geez," he says, annoyed. "Is there anyone you like?"

"Yes," I say. "You. Only you."

After that I don't hear anything more.

I'm awakened by the wind coming in the open door. Volker gives me his hand.

"We're home," he says. "Or do you want to sleep in the car?"

I take his hand and let myself be pulled out of the car. Then he lets go again quickly.

Then don't, I think.

We walk up the stone steps to the front door. His keys jingle. Inside I brace myself with one hand on the wall and work at my shoelaces with the other.

At some point I realize Volker is standing next to me. And that he hasn't turned on any lights.

I lose my balance and my forehead lands on his shoulder. His shirt smells good, though it's sweaty. I like the mix of sweat, cologne, and gasoline scents. The smell of the hospital is in there, too, along with cigarettes from the restaurant earlier tonight and a touch of alcohol.

I rub my forehead on his shoulder.

Volker tussles my hair, pushes me upright, and turns on the light.

Then don't, I think again, turning my back to him and walking slowly up the stairs.

He passes me and turns into the kitchen.

I stop there, too.

I lean against the wall and watch as he pops open a bottle of red wine and pours himself a glass. He empties it and refills it. And again. And again.

Then he notices me.

"Would you like some?" he asks. "Or have you had enough for tonight?"

"More than enough," I say. "Actually, I don't drink."

"That's a shame," he says. "Why not?"

"I don't know," I say. "Maybe because I come from a country where so many people drink themselves to death."

The glass clinks as Volker puts it down.

"You're still young," he says and walks past me out of the kitchen. "You'll change your mind a few more times."

I don't think so, but I don't say that to him.

I walk behind him as if on a leash. Finally we come to the door behind which his bedroom must be. He goes in and doesn't notice that I follow him. In bare feet I'm very quiet.

He sits down on his bed and holds his head in his hands.

"It's a double bed," I say, surprised. Not sure what I had expected.

He looks up, startled. It's dark; he probably can't even make me out.

"You?" he says. "You again?"

I sit down next to him. I can feel the warmth of his hips next to mine. He doesn't move away.

I'm not sure exactly what happens next. But he's holding my head with both hands. He kisses me on the mouth, harder than I had expected, pushing me into the pillows. His fingers run through my hair for a tantalizingly long time. I suppress my nervous shivers and press back, running my hand along his back where his shirt has ridden up.

And then it stops feeling good to me anymore.

His kisses are too fast and aggressive. I don't like it that his watch scratches my skin through my sweater and that his other hand is pulling my hair. I get the feeling he is thinking of somebody else.

It's been a long time since I was in such a ridiculous situation.

He grunts in my ear. The booze on his breath makes it hard for me to get air. I try to squirm away, but he follows determinedly, relentlessly. I roll away again and again and each time he comes after me and wraps me in his arms.

He probably thinks it's just a game, and that he's supposed to chase me.

I'm not sure how to tell him I don't want to play anymore.

It's not that I don't still like him. But I want him to let me go.

But I don't have the heart to shove him away or to ram my knee between his legs. I still like him too much for that, even if his magic is quickly fading.

I roll around the entire bed until I'm sideways against the wooden headboard. I can't go anywhere else. I turn away from Volker and press my face and hands against the cool wood.

Then he lets go of me.

As I look with surprise over my shoulders, he is sitting there rubbing his face. "I'm sorry," he says in a gravelly voice. "I'm so sorry. Please forgive me. Did I scare you?"

I pull myself away from the headboard and sit up warily.

"Why would that scare me?" I say. "I'm not that easily scared."

"Please forgive me," he says. "I shouldn't have done that. What a night."

He sounds horrified. He won't stop rubbing his face and holding his head in his hands.

"Nothing happened," I say. "Everything's all right."

Please forgive me," he repeats. I'm beginning to get tired of his apologies.

"My god," I say, "it's fine. I started it, after all."

"I nearly could have . . . ," he says, shuddering.

"No, you couldn't have," I say calmly. "I know how to defend myself."

"You do?" he asks, turning his ashen face toward me. "Where'd you learn that?"

"Volker," I say wearily, "you really don't want to know all that, do you?"

He doesn't answer.

I pull the covers out from under me and get under them. Grab the nearest pillow and shove it under my head. It's a joy just to lie like this in a nice, soft bed. The corners of my mouth turn upward into—I can't suppress it—an inappropriately sunny smile.

"What are you planning?" Volker asks hoarsely.

"I want to sleep," I say.

"Here?" He sounds totally spent now.

"Yes," I say. "You can be sure I'll never sleep alone in this house. Always something going on here. It's almost like at home."

"And me?" asks Volker. "Where am I supposed to go?"

"There's enough room," I say. "I'll keep my clothes on just so there are no misunderstandings."

"You must be crazy," he says.

I smile in the darkness.

"I bet you'll leave now," I say. "I bet you don't trust yourself—because you're afraid of me."

"You've just lost that bet," Volker says. "Give me back my pillow. I won't sleep well otherwise. Take the other one."

"You know what, Volker," I say just before I fall asleep.

"What," he murmurs from a yard away.

"I thought I was already old," I say and yawn, causing the sentence to come out wrong. I start over: "I thought there was no difference between me and adults. Between me and you, for instance."

"Uh-huh."

"But now I get it. When you're old, you do things differently. At a different tempo. I'm not old yet. For me, it has to go very differently."

"What?" Volker mumbles. "What are you talking about?"

"Sex," I say.

"Those are tough thoughts," says Volker. "What a fucked up night. Quiet now. Let's get some sleep."

I'm soon awake again.

Volker has a clock in his room. It's seven in the morning when I sit up. I'm wired but wrecked at the same time. It's light outside. The chirps of birds waft in through the partly open window. The sun shines on Volker's sleeping face. He looks tired and gray.

He's lying on his back, his mouth half-open, his face slack, a hand tucked behind his head. He's no longer a young man. I can see that clearly this morning.

Something starts to well up and gnaw at me. A feeling I recognize and hate like the plague. A feeling called pity. I don't like the image of Volker racing down the autobahn in the middle of the night with Felix, waiting in the hallway of the hospital, and driving home alone.

Who could possibly leave someone like that, I think. Someone with graying hair, someone good-looking and sophisticated and funny. How can you just abandon your child, especially when he's so sick? A red-haired kid with freckles and a white scar beneath his T-shirt.

Easy.

Then I think of something and jump up, kick myself for my inconsiderateness as Volker stirs, and then tiptoe out of the room. The wood floor is warm and smooth underfoot. And with no shoes on there's no squeaking noise as I walk on it. I run into the guest room, remembering how just a few hours earlier I had been crying and stumbling around screaming for Volker. It all seems like a distant nightmare, something I dreamed years ago.

But Felix is lying in the hospital right now. Or sitting up, staring out the window, upset, shoving aside his breakfast tray.

My mobile is under my pillow. I hold it up in front of my face and see exactly what I feared I would. Eleven missed calls since last night. I didn't have it with me at the cinema, and I was distracted afterwards.

I know something else has happened. As if the terrible night is not yet over.

All the calls are from home.

I dial the number. My hand is shaking. It rings once. Then Maria answers.

"Hello?" she says in a scared tone. Wide awake.

"Maria," I whisper loudly, as if Felix is sleeping next to me and I'm afraid I'll wake him. "Maria, has something happened?"

"Sascha," she says, and starts to cry.

I start to shiver. "Maria," I say woodenly, remaining oddly calm. "What's going on?"

She sobs and gulps.

"Maria," I scream, "what is it? Something with Anton? Alissa? What happened to them? An accident? Appendicitis? Is one of them in the hospital? Was Vadim released? Maria, say something, or . . . or I'll come home."

"Sascha," she says, choke up, "please come back, my dear."

"Tell me what's going on. Have you forgotten how to talk?"

"Please come home."

"Maria, you are driving me nuts." I try to think of all the words I've seen written on derelict walls in Moscow or scrawled in the halls of the Emerald. Words that would have me thrown out of the Alfred Delp School for uttering. "Listen, you aborted fetus," I begin, "you need to tell me what the hell happened!"

The longer Maria listens to me, the calmer she gets.

"Alexandra," she finally says severely, sniffling one last time, "you need to tell me when you are coming home."

"Where are Anton and Alissa?" I scream. I jump up and want to run somewhere and do something.

"In their beds," Maria says grandly. "Where else would they be?"

"What are they doing?" I ask like an idiot.

"Sleeping," she says. "What did you think?"

"Are they sick?"

"What?" she says. "No, they are healthy to the core. Anton did all his homework by himself. He got a hundred percent on his math homework. I couldn't understand the others. Alissa wrote her name with only one 'S.'"

"She's got it tough with that name," I say.

"Grigorij doesn't come over anymore," Maria says softly.

"Oh," I say. "Why not?"

"When will you be home?" asks Maria. "I tried to reach you all night—I was so worried."

My worries instantly melt away.

"You only called," I say out of the blue, "because Anton brought a letter home from school and wouldn't translate it and you want to know what it says."

Maria sighs. "That, too."

"I'll come home," I say. "Maybe even today."

Then she starts to cry again—this time from happiness. It's very quiet, but I hear it and hang up quickly.

"Families are so difficult," I say later to Volker as he's packing up Felix's notebook computer and a few DVDs.

"Yes," Volker says. "Families are walking natural disasters. In my next life I want to come back as a Buddhist monk. No attachments, no possessions, no hair. What about you?"

"President of the United States. I thought Felix was coming home today?"

"My experience tells me otherwise," Volker says. "They probably didn't want to tell him the truth yesterday for fear that he'd get upset and smash their expensive equipment. From your bed straight to the hospital—that's a tough transition. He'll have settled down by this morning, I hope. Do you really want to go home already?"

"What I'd really like to do," I say, "is go someplace far

away. An island, surrounded by nothing but ocean. Palm trees stretching up to the sky. Seagulls crying, white sand, mosquitoes, sunburn."

"And Bacardi," Volker says.

"Why Bacardi?" I ask.

"Because they have a commercial just like the scene you're describing. Dancing girls in grass skirts. You'd look good in one."

"I can't dance," I say.

"Even so," says Volker. He turns the "Cider House Rules" DVD around in his hands. "Felix used to love this movie," he says. "He had a crush on the blonde in it—Charlize Theron. Do you know if he still likes it?"

"He's fallen for the other girl in it—the brunette," I say. "But I can't answer the question. Things change so fast, and people's tastes even faster."

"Yeah, yeah," Volker says, sighing like an old man.

"Felix is going to be disappointed you're gone," he says without looking at me. "At least, I assume."

"Say hello from me," I suggest.

"I will," Volker says. "And I'll tell him you cried when you left and kissed his photo. That you stole one of his sweaty T-shirts out of the laundry as a memento. No, better yet, that I sold you the T-shirt for a bunch of money. That you'll be sitting at home by the phone. He's going to hate me for letting you leave."

"Volker," I say, "you're just buttering me up."

He stretches out his hand and runs it through my hair.

"I see a lot of your mother in you," he says.

I open the apartment door and put down my backpack. The place smells like home fries and onions. I love potatoes and onions. The water is running in the bathroom. I can hear Anton and Alissa arguing in their room. "That was my card, you buttfucker," says Alissa. "Scum," retorts Anton.

I can't stop grinning.

Suddenly they quiet down.

"I heard something," says Anton. "Did you hear anything?"

"Yeah," Alissa says. "Maybe."

I don't move. I can't see them but I can picture the look they have on their faces right now. How they are now standing on their tiptoes, holding each other's hands, and creeping toward the hallway with big eyes.

The door opens.

And then I hear it—deafening. Like a drum roll and a standing ovation at a major premiere. Like the roar of the crowd at a soccer match after a particularly spectacular goal.

"Sascha!" they scream and throw themselves at me.

I have the best grade point average in my entire class. "What odd grades," says Maria. "This funny point system. Always fifteen points. It's hard to keep them straight on the page. Why can't it be as easy as it is back home: one through five. You'd have all fives. People would call you a well-rounded five-star student."

"You're well-rounded," I say.

Alissa jumps on my back and hangs from my shoulders.

"When I grow up I want to have three babies," she says loudly in my ear.

"Don't shout," I say. "Three—that's a lot."

"I want a lot," Alissa says. "Do I have to couple three times?"

"Oh boy," says Maria, suddenly getting very uncomfortable.

"No, you don't have to," I say in a strong tone. "You don't have to do anything you don't want to do."

"I can have babies without a partner?"

"Yes, of course," I say. "What does the one thing have to do with the other?"

"I knew it!" says Alissa. "See Maria, I knew you didn't need a partner. Do I have to kiss someone?"

"Well, you don't have to," I say, "but it doesn't hurt."
"We'll see," she says. "I'll kiss you, okay? Or Anton."
"Fine," I say.

The phone rings that night.
"Sascha," Maria calls. "Phone!"
"Answer it," I say. "Push the green button."
"It's better if you do, dear."
"Maria, I'm downloading something."
"What?"
"Green button! You can do it! You're annoying, Maria."
"No, you," she says, genuinely upset. I jump up from my chair, stumble over a cord, ripping it out of the socket, and reach for the phone in Maria's hand.

There's only one person who would let the phone ring that long.

"Hello there, speedy," says Felix. "Explain math to me. I don't understand it at all."

"Email me your homework," I say. "I'll have a look."

"By the way, I wrote a poem for you," Felix says, as if the homework is my problem, not his. "Because you're so cultured. Listen." He clears his throat theatrically and reads with gravitas:

Let's sit together in the kitchen
Where sweet is the smell of kerosene white
Let's open the bento box of sushi
And an entire flask of gin
And then we'll pack the big suitcases
So full they'll almost burst
Strap on our wings and lift off
Heading for distant southern atolls.

"Is it better than the last one? You shouldn't laugh when I'm reading a poem to you. That's not fair. I'm still learning.

You're going to put me off writing. I'll be poetically impotent . . . Alexandra!"

I'm bending over because I'm laughing so hard my stomach hurts. I wipe tears from my eyes.

"Where did you find that?" I ask.

"I wrote it for you. Just now. No, actually, last night."

"Stop talking shit. It's a parody of Osip Mandelstam."

"What-stam?"

"Where did you find it?"

"Online," says Felix, defeated. "Some poetry site. You jerk."

"Hang on," I say, "I'll grab the book."

"Unbelievable," Felix grumbles while I squat in front of the bookshelf where my mother's books of poetry are shelved. "I mean, I probably should have figured you would have read that Shakespeare sonnet. But this? Something totally obscure? How could I expect you to know that?"

"Pure coincidence, my hero," I say flipping through a thin book. "But that is a pretty well-known poem. I guess I must have been listening when she read it to me all those times. Ah, here it is:

Let's sit together in the kitchen
Where sweet is the smell of kerosene white.

"Obviously from here on it's different—instead of sushi there's a sharp knife, a loaf of bread, ropes and baskets . . . "

"How exciting," says Felix.

"And about getting away. They want to go to the train station. They're probably scared of getting arrested—this was written in 1931."

"Hey, speaking of getting away," says Felix quickly, as soon as he's listened to my full explanation, "you know why I'm calling? Volker wants to know if you'll go to Tenerife with us during summer vacation."

"What did you say?" I ask, because I'm still reading the book. "Tenerife?"

"Yeah, Tenerife. It's an island. In the Canaries. Surrounded by the ocean. We're going there. Come with us."

"Who suggested it?" I say suspiciously. "Did Volker really say I should go along?"

"Of course."

"Did he tell you to ask me?"

"Well, okay, it was my idea. But he liked the idea. He said he'd like to have somebody there to keep me out of his hair. So he wouldn't have to deal with my permanent bad mood. He said he'd pay somebody a good hourly wage to do it, just to save his vacation."

"Is that how he put it?" I ask. "Really?"

"What's with all the stupid questions? Of course he wants you to come. He likes you a lot. It would be two weeks. If you came along it would make it almost bearable."

"Wow, what a charming way to put it," I say absentmindedly.

I picture myself lying on the beach between Felix and Volker. How I casually put my foot near Volker's and stick the bottle of sun-cream in the sand as a protective barrier against Felix. I can hear the crash of the waves and the cry of the seagulls. And I hear the tune from the Bacardi ad.

"Why are you laughing?" asks Felix.

"It's nothing," I say. "I'll think it over, okay?"

"Just don't think about it for too long or else Volker will be gone."

"And so will you."

"No. If you don't go, I'm not going either."

"Don't start, Felix," I say, looking at the clock. I still have to fill out the applications for my advanced placement courses.

"By the way," says Felix. "We haven't practiced in a while."

"What do you mean practice?" I say. "I'm sure by now you are a regular Pieter Brueghel."

"Who?" says Felix. "Why are you always trying to piss me off?"

"I'm not trying to piss you off," I say. "I just meant that by now you are a master. Let's talk tomorrow, okay?"

"Tomorrow?" he says. The disappointment in his voice barely registers. "You always say that. And then you never have time."

"Jesus, I do have things to do," I say.

Felix is silent. Hurt.

"Hey," I say, "no crying, my dear. A little tan will do you good."

"I just burn," Felix says.

"Then I'll put cream on you."

"I'd rather be the one creaming on you."

"You're annoying, Felix. Listen, I have a job. I can't go away."

"A job?" says Felix. "Why didn't you say that right away? Can't you just ditch it for a while?"

"I should have told you right off the bat. I just forgot."

"How stupid do you think I am?"

"What happens if you have breathing problems on Tenerife?"

"Why don't you . . . "

"Why don't you just tell me what happens."

Felix suddenly loses interest in the conversation.

"Okay, I'll talk to you tomorrow," he says.

"Felix, I hate it when you don't answer me."

"Why do you ask anyway? Are you worried about me?"

"What a question," I say. "What do you want to hear? Yes! Yes! Yes! I am so worried about you."

"The deal is," he says with annoyance in his voice, "we always have to stay near a hospital. I have no idea if there are cities on Tenerife, but there must be hospitals, because otherwise Volker would never suggest going there. It's that simple. He'll bring medicine and a copy of my medical records and instructions from our hospital on what to do in the case of an emergency. Normally any old hospital can handle it. And we can always reach my doctor by phone in case they can't figure out what to do. What else do you want to know?"

"Thanks for putting my mind at ease," I say. "But now tell me the truth."

"Did I mention that I can't stand you?" says Felix. "Seriously cannot stand you?"

"Yep," I say. "Lots of times."

He slams down the phone. Probably on the table so I can hear it. Only afterwards does he hang up.

I go down to the third floor to pick up Alissa from her friend Katja's place.

The walls are thin in the Emerald. By the time I get down to the fifth floor, I can hear Alissa's voice. It's high and piercing, loud and happy. A future soprano, as my mother always used to say back when Alissa was really little and would screech for her bottle. "Sounds more like something on an ultrasonic wavelength," I would answer. "Like a dolphin. Bores into your head."

I sound completely different. My voice is lower and scratchier. "Because I smoked when I was pregnant with you," my mother used to say.

"I won't smoke if I ever get pregnant."

"I guess you're smarter than me."

"Which is exactly why I won't get pregnant."

"That's what I used to say. Until I had you. Then I realized it was a joy worth repeating."

"And you smoked your way through it."

"I'm really sorry about that, sweetie. I would do it differently now. You could have gotten kidney damage from it."

"And I'm stuck with a baritone because you smoked."

"More like a tenor. Your father had a baritone. You should have heard him lecture. I went once. I understood only one word."

"What word?"

"And."

"You know what? This doesn't interest me."

"That's what he used to say. About everything I told him."

Anton's voice isn't particularly high or low. He has hardly any voice at all. Just a quiet rustling. Anton is practically invisible—thin and blond and weak and fearful.

Anton, I think. My Anton. I would give you my voice and my brains if I thought it would help you come to grips with everything. But I don't think it would help you. I'm so scared for you. I know you're not going to make it. If you're lucky you'll end up like Harry.

And if you end up like Vadim, I'll kill you.

Back then, the time when your parents came home from that first parent-teacher meeting, you had such a fucked-up evening. Your father was so angry at you, and he kept yanking on his tie—the one your mother had put so much energy into tying—as if it were trying to strangle him.

The polka dot pattern of that tie is forever burned into my memory. Along with Vadim's face above that pattern, full of rage, flushed, his eyes squinting.

And words, his words.

"How dare you—*my* son—awful in school—don't talk—you dimwit, you failure, you pussy—what an embarrassment—little idiot—shut your mouth, you—nobody asked you to say a word—I'm warning you, I'm doing the talking here—tell that brat she better shut up or there will be consequences—you'll never, never, never amount to anything—in the old days your type would have been . . . "

Anton was cowering in the corner of the sofa, light eyebrows, lips drained of blood, his face colorless, his wide-open eyes trained on Vadim—who loomed hulking in the middle of the room, gesticulating, spitting out his words along with saliva.

And then his hand, with its short fingers, gripping his leather belt and opening it with a few quick motions, the hiss of the belt cutting through the air and my memory of his words: "Back in the old days, in the army, we would fill our buckles with lead and, man, did that crack your skull." Chuckling as he did it.

I misunderstood, thinking he had lead in this belt buckle and was about to crack open Anton's blond head.

Of course it was just a normal belt, a normal belt that whipped me across my face when I stepped between Anton and Vadim—not that it felt good. Everyone screamed except Anton, who I thought was dead by that point, keeled over in the corner of the sofa.

And I thought that was just normal, nothing shocking, the nature of a situation like this, just like the pain burning across my face. Until I realized my mother was screaming, too. That was something I couldn't comprehend.

She never screamed. Never.

And now she was in Vadim's face yelling, shouting that it was over, done, finished; that they were through, there would be no more agonizing over it; that he would never, ever hurt a child again; that he was leaving the apartment right this second; that she was filing for divorce—out! Out!

And Vadim dropped the hand with the belt to his side and listened with his mouth agape.

Out!

And I thought that he would whip her now, and that I needed to think of something fast to keep him from killing her. Where was the phone? Mother was so disorganized and never put the handset back on its cradle.

Out!

Then Vadim fell to his knees and started to cry, still clutching the belt in one hand while the other quivered in the air.

The scene made me sick.

I looked away, at my mother. But she didn't look at me. She was still looking at Vadim, her eyes tightly squinting. And in her hand was the phone.

"Out," she said, almost whispering. "I've already dialed the number. I don't want to hear another word."

Vadim had difficulty standing up, nearly falling over, fighting to regain his balance. You could tell he realized how absurd he looked at that moment.

"Now?" he said, just as quietly, trying to read her face. If he was able to read it, he didn't like what he saw in it.

She nodded and put the phone to her ear. Vadim shook his head no, wiped his nose on his shirtsleeve and began to put his belt back through the loops of his pants, slowly, having difficulty, finally leaving it be, walking past her and out of the room with his belt dangling. I didn't even realize that I had jumped to my feet again, ready for the possibility he would try to hit her.

At first I couldn't believe he was gone. Until I heard the front door close, I thought he was waiting for us in the entryway.

When I finally came to my senses again, my mother was already sitting on the couch with Anton on her lap. His eyes were still wide open, and his face was smeared with brown from the chocolate she was stuffing in his mouth like a life-saving medicine.

I looked at them and blinked uncomprehendingly until my mother said, "He did it. He did it again. He hurt my child."

And I answered automatically, "Don't exaggerate. He didn't even touch Anton."

"I'm not talking about Anton," said my mother. "He hit you. He dared to hit you."

And as I sat down next to them and took a piece of chocolate for myself, she said, "He's never coming back here."

And fifteen minutes later she said, "Where did you get the nerve, Sascha? Are you not afraid of anything at all? How is that possible? How did you get that way?"

I felt the chocolate melting in my hand. I didn't even want to eat it. So I wiped it off on my pants.

"Never again," my mother said, hugging Anton. "Never again, it's over, done."

"Me!" shrieked Alissa. I could clearly hear her from the staircase. "Me, me, me!"

I'm not worried about Alissa. She's been good to go since she came into this world. She was born in the ambulance because my mother didn't make it to the hospital in time. A screaming red bundle with a head of pitch-black hair and a startlingly observant look in her dark blue eyes. Pretty as a picture and full of energy. I held her, newly born, in my arms as my mother, no longer pregnant, took the elevator back up to our place and got into her bed. I never saw her so happy again.

"A girl, Sascha," she kept saying. She hadn't let them tell her in advance what she was having. She was drunk with joy. "You know what, Sascha? I never said anything, but I really wanted it to be a girl. Girls have it so much easier in life."

"I'm not sure about that," I said, looking at Alissa's wrinkled red face. Alissa looked at me, too, studying, skeptical. And when we put her in her crib, she would close her eyes and open her mouth and scream until the walls of the entire Emerald shook.

"It's all right," I said, "No need to get out of bed. I can handle it. I can hold her. She likes it in my arms."

"I want to hold her, too," said my mother. "Give her to me. Give her to me, I said. Who gave birth to her—you or me?"

My little sister never wanted to be put down. Within a few days, we were all doing her bidding. Even Vadim overcame his disappointment at not getting a son worthy of carrying on his name, turned down the TV, and carried Alissa around until her diapers were full—"baby shit is not something for a man to handle." He even said he saw his grandfather in her tiny features, started calling her "his princess" and "snuggle-bunny," and bought her a doll in a red dress.

I blow on my pointer finger and put it on the doorbell.

I'm excited to see Alissa again.

Peter the Great comes to the door. I haven't forgotten that little Katja is his sister. I just didn't think about it.

"Hi," I say. He nods and lets me into the apartment.

"Your little sister," he says instead of a greeting, "is like a siren. My ears are ringing."

He stretches out his arm, leans against the wall, and looks me up and down. His facial expression is hard to read.

I don't look away. It doesn't go unnoticed.

He really is gigantic. Six and a half feet of muscle and acne, adrenalin, and testosterone, and whatever it is you get when you sniff glue, all packed into oddly tight jeans and a white T-shirt. The Marlon Brando of our Russian Ghetto. Long black eyelashes that give his face a feminine note. Which is probably why he lifts weights so obsessively. Light blue eyes, red lips that crinkle easily, a thick gold chain around his neck, and an even thicker one around his wrist. A fat ring on his pinkie and tattoos on his upper arm. There's the obligatory naked woman—with no head—as well as an eagle and some symbol I don't recognize.

No, he doesn't sniff glue, I think. His eyes are too clear and observant. Maybe a couple of beers and a joint, but only on weekends. He can restrain himself. Probably drinks protein shakes and pops vitamins.

I think he's younger than me. I'm pretty sure he's only sixteen.

There sure are a lot of sixteen-year-old boys in this world.

"How's it going?" he says.

"Fine," I say. "You?"

A door flies open and Alissa comes stumbling out. She's pulling a toy wagon with three Barbies lying in it. She sees me, shouts a greeting, and pulls the wagon past me and Peter and on into another room.

"Come on, Katja," she screams. "Where are you?"

Katja comes out of the doorway. She's a year older than Alissa, already five. Her face is round. Her pink tights are twisted around. And too small. Katja's one of those chubby kids who can't help bringing attention on herself—the wrong kind. For instance, I have rarely seen her without a chocolate bar in her mouth. Even now her mouth is smeared brown. So is Alissa's.

"Hi, Katja," I say. She jumps, startled, and stares at me. "What are you playing?"

"I don't know," she mumbles.

"What do you mean you don't know? You're one of the ones playing it."

"Formula One," shrieks Alissa from the next room. "We're playing Formula One racing. Come on, Katja."

Katja sticks her thumb in her mouth. Her eyes are the color of water, like Peter's. There must be twenty-six barrettes in her hair.

I wink at her. She takes her thumb out of her mouth and hides her hand behind her back.

"How come you never come up to our place?" I ask. "I think Alissa would like it."

Katja says nothing and looks over at Peter. Peter looks at me from above and likewise says nothing.

"I'm not allowed," mumbles Katja.

"Why aren't you allowed?" I ask. "Who said you weren't allowed?"

"Mommy," she says.

I raise my face to look directly at Peter.

"Why isn't she allowed?" I ask. "Does your mother think we eat children?"

The corners of Peter's mouth turn up. "How should I

know," he says. "As far as I'm concerned she can visit you any-time she wants. I'd enjoy the peace and quiet."

"I'm not allowed," Katja says more stridently.

I kneel down in front of her. "I'll ask your mother if you can, okay?"

She nods. Then she nods again, more vigorously. "I want to see Alissa's robots," she says.

"I'll ask your mother," I repeat. "When will she be home?" I ask, this time directing the question to Peter.

"Forget it," Peter says, stretching and touching the ceiling as he does. "She comes home at seven, but you can save yourself the trouble."

I stand up. I stretch, too, but I only reach the level of his shoulders. "What do you mean?" I ask angrily. "What did we ever do to your mother?"

"You know how they are around here," says Peter. "She's afraid. She was home the night it all went down at your place. I can hardly believe she lets the little runt come over here even. The adults are all so spineless and stupid."

"It was Vadim," I say. "Vadim did the shooting. Not me. Not Maria. Why shouldn't Katja be allowed to come over?"

Peter shrugs his massive shoulders.

"Look, personally I don't give a shit," he says. "But my mother says you can still smell tragedy up on the eleventh floor. She's a bit out there. When she sees a black cat she spits three times over her left shoulder so nothing bad happens to her."

"Is that it?" I ask. "She's just superstitious?"

"I've never asked her," he says, "but if I were in your position, I'd want to move out of that apartment."

"Why?"

"It's poisoned. Somebody was stabbed nine years ago on the eighth floor—you weren't here yet—and to this day there's only one apartment rented out on the entire floor."

"You can't be serious."

"You can still see the blood stains on the floor in front of your apartment."

"That's just dirt."

"Right."

"If your father killed your mother," I say, "would you want to move out of here? The apartment where you lived together with her? The place you call home? And her last home? Would you really split?"

"That would never happen to my mother," Peter says.

That hurts. I only realize after a few seconds that I've clenched my fists so tightly that my fingernails have pierced the skin on my hands. There are several red, crescent-shaped cuts.

"Your mother?" I say. "No, you're right, it would never happen to her."

"What?" says Peter. "What do you mean by that?"

"What did *you* mean?"

And then I realize Peter is smarter than I thought—he doesn't answer.

The children's voices have gone quiet. And I can now hear the music coming out of the open door to Peter's room. I know the song.

*The drunken doctor*
*Told you*
*That you*
*No longer exist.*
*The fire department says*
*Your house*
*Has burned down.*

"No way," I say. "You listen to Nautilus Pompilius?"

"What else am I supposed to listen to?" says Peter, annoyed. "The Lollipops? What's your problem?"

I have no problem. I stand there, try to breathe. Everything swims in front of my eyes.

"You listen to that?" I say pointlessly.

"For god's sake," Peter says, pissed off. "No, I don't listen to it. I eat it."

The song hits me like a punch in the gut.

There's no way Peter really listens to the music of this long-forgotten Russian goth band. My mother liked them. She listened to a lot of rock and pop, as well as chansons and musicals and opera. She never got stuck in any one genre.

How is it possible, I wonder, that here—in an apartment that reeks of coal, that's scrubbed spic and span, a place where every piece of furniture is draped with a doily, where there are plastic flowers in vases on the windowsills, where the walls are covered with the type of horrible pictures of pink children that you can get three-for-ten-bucks at the supermarket, where red-checkered curtains flutter in the wind—that here of all places, this music is played?

*In a strange room*
*With a white ceiling*
*A right to hope*
*And a belief*
*In love.*

I stare at the checkered curtains.

We never had curtains. My mother hated them. It might be the one thing she categorically ruled out. She always wanted to have the windows open. The sun should come in. "Let the sun in and the rain will follow." That's a line from Die Fantischen Vier my mother liked. Yep, she even liked German hip-hop. The first thing Maria did when she arrived was to sew curtains—loudly colored, with giant flowers all over them. She put them up and pulled them closed.

Then I came home from school and she took them down again. Real fast. She made a blouse for herself out of the fabric. And one for Alissa.

Then she quickly took apart Alissa's and turned it into three tops for Alissa's dolls instead.

*The drunken doctor*
*Told you*
*That you*
*No longer exist.*

Peter reaches out with a bulging arm and taps me on the shoulder.

"What?" I say, taking a step back.

"Why don't you come out to Broken Glass Park sometime?" he asks without looking at me. "You know, back in the woods."

"What—where you guys drink and smoke weed and tag-team girls three at a time in the bushes? What would I want to do there?"

"Well, you just explained that yourself."

"I'll pass."

"It's not true about three guys doing girls at the same time. Where did you hear that? That only happened twice—and the girls wanted it."

"Yeah, well, I don't want it."

"Are you scared?"

I go right up to him and stand on my tiptoes.

"Get something straight," I say. "I. Am. Not. Scared. Of. Anything."

"Then come along. What's the problem?"

"You guys make me sick. That's the problem."

"Aha," he says calmly, lowering his head. "You want something better."

"Exactly," I say, and watch as his face changes. As if he's been stung.

Then he gets his facial expression under control again.

"I wouldn't be saying that kind of thing if I were in your situation," he says slowly. "It could come back to haunt you."

"I'm shitting myself. With fear."

"Wise of you."

"Alissa," I say loudly. "How long do I have to wait for you? Let's go home."

No answer.

"Is he a good fuck?" asks Peter suddenly, looking me directly in the eyes.

"Who?" I say, stunned.

"The sugar daddy I saw here, the one who dropped you off. Some old guy with gray hair. I know how you are. You think we're nothing but trash. But in reality you're the worst of all, just a miserable slut. So is he a good fuck?"

"Oh, yeah," I say. "Amazing. I can hardly wait for the next round. Alissa! I'm leaving."

She comes shooting around the corner and grabs my hand with her hot, sticky fingers.

"You can keep the bracelet," she says to Katja, who waves goodbye somewhat lethargically. "I'm giving it to you."

In the elevator she asks, "Who is Vadim?" Then she shouts, "Wait! Let me push the button!"

"Vadim?" I say, hoisting her up so she can reach the button. "Nobody."

I've started running again. My favorite time to run is evenings, when it cools off a little. I run past the supermarket, past a sad old man's pub, through a grove of sycamores, once around the local school, and then into the park and under the underpass. There's almost always a train rushing past overhead.

It's dark and moist under there even in the middle of the

day at the height of the summer. Kids Anton's age are always lighting little fires under here. I always come across little holes in the dirt filled with ash and charred twigs or burnt strips of newspaper.

I saw Anton down here once, too, and I was glad to see there was no fire burning near him. But my relief was premature. Anton was squatting down, busy doing something back in the bushes together with a black-haired boy. He flinched as I came closer and looked over his shoulder.

And I flinched, too, because at his feet was something that looked like a raw steak with fur and tiny feet.

And I thought to myself: I need to toughen up. How am I going to fulfill my mission if this is making me nauseated?

The thing that surprised me most was that Anton was clearly leading this odd operation. The other kid was just watching, and rolled his chocolate-colored eyes as I angrily lit into my little brother.

"Why did you kill this little creature?" I yelled at Anton, who just shrugged and shook his head.

"It was already dead," said the other kid. There was a strange hostility in his pretty, brown saucer eyes, though he looked past me rather than right at me. As if I was too disgusting to look at directly.

"What is that thing anyway? And who are you?"

"I'm Ilhan."

"And what's that?"

"A hamster. Are you blind or something?"

"No," I said. "I'm not blind." Though I wouldn't mind it when faced with this bloody clump of fur.

"Did you kill the hamster, Anton?" I asked in a weak voice. "I don't believe it."

"It was already dead," he mutters.

"Died last night, I'm telling you," said the other boy. "It's my hamster. It belongs to me."

"What the hell are you doing?" I asked with disgust. There was no other way to react—Anton was holding the handle of our kitchen knife in his blood-smeared hand, and the blade was buried in the lump at his feet.

"I'm trying to skin it," Anton mumbled without looking up at me. It was taking every ounce of effort not to throw up on my shoes.

"With your bare hands?" I said.

"How else would you do it?" asked Anton as he gripped the lump with his skinny fingers and tried to pull it open, as stuff oozed from the carcass. The other boy leaned over him, his brow wrinkled with concentration.

"What's that?" asked Anton curiously. "Do you know, Sascha? Have a look."

"I'd rather not," I said faintly. "Maybe another time."

"Is that the heart?" asked Ilhan with interest. I pulled myself together, kneeled down, and took the knife from Anton's hand, gulped, bit my lower lip, and tried to turn the hamster carcass carefully with the blade. Quite a bit of stuff fell out of the body cavity.

Crazy how much fits into such a small animal.

"The heart is very small in a hamster like this," I said, rummaging around inside the carcass with the knife. "This is probably it here. No idea. That big thing there is the intestine."

"And that?"

"Not sure. Probably the kidneys."

"Cool."

"Yuck. All right, Anton, get home, wash your hands. This thing is full of germs. Dead animals are poisonous. Remember that. Wash your hands three times with soap. How can you guys be so stupid and so savage?"

"It was already dead," Anton mumbled.

"We just wanted to dissect it," said Ilhan.

"Look at me when you talk to me—even if your father

doesn't look at your mother when he talks to her," I said. To my surprise he obeyed.

"We were going to stuff it," he explained grudgingly, looking me in the eyes. "Anton said he could do it. I brought gauze from home. And he brought a needle to stitch it back together."

"You thought you could do that?" I asked, perplexed, looking at an increasingly unhappy Anton, who pushed a few strands of blond hair out of his face with his blood-smeared hand. "For the love of god, get your fingers away from your hair."

"Why don't you think I could do it?" asked Anton glumly.

"Aren't you disgusted by it?"

"No, why?"

"Anton!"

"What?"

"I said to get home."

"What are we supposed to do with the hamster?" asked Ilhan.

"Nothing. You can't stuff it. You have to be trained to be able to do that. It's complicated. It'll just rot if you guys try. Disgusting. Throw it away and off you go."

They looked at each other for a long time, Anton and Ilhan. Then Anton sighed and Ilhan looked up with disappointment in his eyes as a train rushed past overhead.

"Let's at least bury it," said Ilhan.

So I squatted down and watched as they dug a hole a few yards deeper into the brush and Anton collected the hamster and its innards with his bare hands and chucked it all into the hole. Ilhan didn't seem to want to touch it. Then they filled in the hole again and decorated the mound with dandelions and lilacs. I watched as Anton then found two sticks and made a cross, with Ilhan helping him.

"Three times with soap," I repeated as they started up the embankment toward broken glass park and the Emerald.

Now I always run past that spot. The dandelions have long since withered and been blown away. I always look off to the side and wonder what the carcass looks like now.

Every time I have to fight the unnatural urge to dig up the hamster and have a look. And every time I tell myself it's probably not even there anymore, as a dog or fox or something will have found it long ago.

Then one time I give in and start to root around in the dirt with a stick.

Just as I'm thinking I must have the wrong spot I find the hole—and its contents exceed all my expectations.

It is full of fat maggots, dozens—no, hundreds. They are all moving, creating a dirty-white writhing mass. It's disgusting. But I count it as a victory of an odd sort.

Because I don't feel nauseated, and that makes me happy.

I've seen enough and I scrape the dirt back over the body, throw the stick into the bushes, and run on.

Beneath the train overpass I see them.

I recognize Peter immediately. He's the biggest. His two buddies are my size. I don't know them. They flank him like two stunted bodyguards.

"Siamese kitty," they say in unison as they block my way. It almost sounds as if they have rehearsed it.

"Let me by," I say. When they don't move, I try to push my way through. But they stand close together, and I can feel their sweaty bodies on my bare arms. Then I feel their fingers as they restrain me.

"Paws off me," I say. "Wash yourselves before you touch me."

One starts to laugh. He sounds drunk. Sure enough, he can barely stand up straight.

"What a bitch," says the other one to Peter. "I love bitches."

"Go fuck yourself," I say. "And before you do, take your paws off me."

"Fear?" asks Peter, smiling at me. Actually in a fairly friendly manner. "Paws off," he says to the one who is still standing up straight. "She's a good girl."

The guy lets go of me.

But then Peter blocks my way. I take a step to the right and he steps in my way. I take a step to the left and he steps in my way. He follows me like a mirror image. And he won't stop smiling. His shoulders gleam as if they are oiled up.

"Why haven't you come to broken glass park?" he asks. "I invited you, after all."

"It stinks too bad for me there," I say. "Everything stinks there."

"Even me?" asks Peter, getting right in my face. I wrinkle up my nose. He seems to use the same cheap cologne as Maria. A pint at a time. The Emerald scent.

"You?" I say. "You stink the worst of all."

I duck just in time to avoid his fist. One of Peter's buddies sits down on the grass. The other snickers.

"Hitting a girl," I say. "How very courageous of you."

"Girls like you need to be smacked around," he says, breathing heavily. "And ones like your mother. It's fucked up that you're not scared of anything. I think we need to change that."

He motions to the buddy who is still standing. He moves without a word. In an instant he's right behind me and I can feel his breath on my neck. His hot hand reaches under my hoodie and a wave of nausea washes over me.

I ram my elbows into his ribs, rip myself free, jump to the side, and bend down. I had already seen it gleaming—an empty brown beer bottle. I grab it and brandish it above my head.

The guy lying in the grass whistles.

"Come on," says Peter, trying to sound nonchalant. It's hard to pull off with his teeth gritted. "Don't play games. You're not stupid—you can see you don't have a chance. Come on, just once, then we'll let you go. You only have to do me. Even a rich sugar daddy gets boring after a while. If you want, the guys here can take a little walk while we're at it. This is a one-time offer."

"Why me?" I ask. "Where are all your blondes with their huge tits? Have you already nailed them all?"

"Pretty much," he says. "A man needs variety. There's something about you I like."

"I only sleep with guys who can read," I sneer. It's like I'm possessed. "Which means you're out, dear Peter. I'm afraid welfare checks and broken German just don't get me off."

His mouth clenches tightly. It's very quiet. Just a few chirps in the background.

"You are fucked now," he says.

"No, you are, Peter. I'll do it. Anybody who comes near me I'll cut open their face."

"I'm going to make your life a living hell," he says quietly.

"Too late," I say. "It already is. Let me through, you fucking asshole."

He puts out his arms. I slash at his face with the bottle.

But I've misjudged it.

The bottle doesn't break. It's still whole. And it flies out of my hand, slipping between my sweaty fingers. I've barely hurt Peter at all. He just grunts, puts his hand up to his face, and then lunges at me. I'm thrown back by the weight of his body and my head hits the wall.

That's when I begin to scream. At first I don't know myself what I am screaming. It's a word. A name.

I am screaming for Volker.

He's startled on the phone. Probably because he's never experienced me in a state like this. I can't even say a word. All I can do is cry. My pillow is soaked with tears and snot. I think I've been grinding my teeth on it, too.

"I'm on my way," he says finally, sounding unsure. It snaps me back together a little.

I wipe my face and press the phone to my ear.

"Not a chance in hell," I say. "It's too late anyway."

"I don't understand what happened," he says helplessly. "Were you attacked? Did somebody do something to you? Are you crazy—walking around there by yourself at night? What are you thinking?"

"Stop yelling at me," I say.

"What happened?" he asks again. "Would you tell me?"

"They let me go," I say. "I called your name. Really loud. Did you hear it there in Bad Soden? Maybe they thought someone was coming. They tried to cover my mouth. I bit that hand so hard it bled. The bottle didn't break, Volker. Those fucking bottles are so strong."

"You should go to a doctor," Volker says. "I think you might be hurt."

"No, I'm not," I say.

"I'm on the way," he says. "I'll pick you up. It's been a while since we saw each other anyway."

"No."

"Why not?"

"I can't leave my children alone."

"Then they should come, too."

"I still can't."

"Why, for god's sake?"

"You know why."

"No, I don't."

"Yes, you do."

"No," he says rigidly. "I have no idea."

He always says that—he doesn't know what I'm talking about. He's never uttered a word about what happened between us. He is very thoughtful and caring. But he doesn't want to acknowledge that night.

"Don't cry," he says quietly. "If nothing happened . . . you're very lucky. Thank god. Promise me that in the future you'll be more careful. That you won't go wandering around that ghetto at night. I understand that you've had a shock. You should talk to a therapist about it."

"Volker," I say, "you're talking bullshit."

"True," he says. "But I can't think of anything better to say. I'd love to give you a hug. But my arms aren't long enough to reach. I don't know what I can do for you."

"You saved me tonight," I say.

"I'm sorry?"

"Your name saved me."

He is quiet for a suspiciously long time.

"Don't tell Felix about this," I say.

"I wasn't planning to," says Volker.

"Do you know why I'm crying?" I say. "Listen to me. I didn't save her. Not her and not Harry. But I could have. If I had gotten between them. If I hadn't just stood there in the door with my arms crossed, annoyed. I should have done something."

"You're crazy," says Volker. "If you had, we wouldn't be on the phone right now."

"I could have done it. I could do anything. I could. Before. I wasn't afraid of anything. Until tonight. Now I'm afraid again. I'm afraid of being afraid."

"Thank god," says Volker muffled.

"I'm so afraid."

"Oh, sweetheart."

"I can't take it here anymore."

"Where?"

"Here at the Emerald. I've always been attached to this apartment. But I just can't take it any longer. I want to get out of here. Maybe I'll move downtown—I need to finish school. I hate the Emerald. I hate the people here. There's nothing I can do about it, and nothing they can do either. They're a bunch of impoverished pigs. And they are only getting poorer. I provoke them. They let it slide, but secretly they hate me. I hate the way it smells here, the stench. I hate the laundry hanging from the balconies. I hate the satellite dishes . . . ”

“Those are everywhere. Please don’t cry. I can’t comfort you from afar. We’ll take care of it, okay? As soon as we’re back from vacation. It’s no problem at all. I’ll be happy when you’re out of there. And speaking of vacation, are you coming with us?”

“Better not,” I say.

“Why not?”

“You know why.”

“No, I don’t. Think about it.”

I love you, I think to myself, are the saddest words in the world.

He’s gone during July. With Felix. It’s scorching hot. The Emerald holds the heat into the wee hours until it starts to get light again.

Maria complains every morning that she won’t make it through the day. The daily calendar for Russian Orthodox housewives supplies her with new recipes for cold soups and warm facial masks. One big cucumber suffices for both.

She found a broad straw hat on the street, only slightly crumpled, and wears it whenever she leaves the house. It makes her look like a giant mushroom.

I’ve shown her the way to the public pool and gotten her a season pass. In the morning she packs a cooler with buttered rolls and mineral water and grapes and watermelon and sour pickles and apple cake and heads off to the pool with Anton, who’s on summer break. He dives and swims with his school friends while Maria sits with her straw hat on in the shadow of an oak tree, fans herself with the pages of an advertising circular, and wonders at the fact that every wasp in the city seems to be buzzing around her cooler. In the middle of the day Anton and Maria come home, eat cold soup, pick up Alissa from kindergarten, and then they go back to the pool all together.

I'm a lot friendlier to Maria now—I think she's a real martyr. I even complimented her on her turquoise bathing suit once; it was the only one in the outlet store that wasn't too small for her. I worry about her a little in the evenings, when she sits sweating in front of the TV, her face bright red, wheezing like a hippo. "Us people from Novosibirsk just weren't made for this kind of weather," she says. "We just melt."

And that's what it looks like.

"Don't forget to drink a lot of water," I say, wondering silently whether Vadim has any more cousins if this one expires.

I'm happy that Anton has finally earned his swimming certification—the "little seahorse" badge, they call it—meaning I don't have to stay with him in the kiddie pool.

It's too loud and shrill there. As soon as I smell the chlorine, my feet start to itch. I have no more desire to sit on the "family" lawn, where little kids will drip their ice cream on my towel and bigger kids will kick their soccer ball in my face, than I do to hang out on the lawn where all the recent graduates of the local high school and trade school smoke, spit in the grass, and tussle with their squeaky girlfriends.

It all makes me sick.

Peter's there, too. He doesn't look at me and I don't look at him. Even when we occasionally pass each other on stairs back at the Emerald.

When I'm home alone, I pull down the shades and listen to Eminem. I turn it up really loud. I don't care if the entire building can hear it.

I used to be embarrassed to like Eminem. I would never have admitted it. In the event someone asked me about it, I always had an answer at the ready: it was Anton's music.

But of course nobody ever asked me. All sorts of stuff blasts through the Emerald and blends together in the staircases—military marches, techno, easy listening, old Russian songs, the Moonlight Sonata, "Jesus Christ Superstar," Bizet's "Carmen," static-filled radio shows ("and now a beautiful song for faithful listener Lydia, from Irkutsk—happy fifty-third birthday"), heavy metal. That along with all kinds of live noises—shattered dishes, stifled gasps, laughs, political discussions, and first and foremost fights, which drown out everything else. "Shut the hell up, you bitch, you've ruined my entire life . . . "—"Me? Your life? Did you all hear that?"

And Eminem.

And me.

Because the rapper from Detroit and I often sing duets. And these days I'm comfortable with the fact that I like him. I even wear a T-shirt sometimes with an image of him on it—he's loading a revolver, grimacing, bleached hair, tattoos, yes sir.

He's the only artist I've been able to listen to in the last two years—for hours on end. And the only one I really believe, the only one who has lived what he describes in his music. I like the fact that he became a father at a young age, and that he has adopted children. I get emotional following his saga in the media, his divorces and marriages, all with the one woman, and his battle with his own family. And I feel sorry for him, because in comparison to the 8 Mile area where he grew up, the Emerald is a palace. I'd rather live here than in a trailer park.

Anyway, we sing together a lot, him singing his lyrics and me singing mine. But the melody is the same, and so is the basic feeling. But we each have our own themes, and like parallel lines we'll never intersect.

*I'm sorry, Mama*, says Eminem.
You'll be sorry, Vadim, says Sascha.
*I never meant to hurt you.*
I'm really going to hurt you.
*I never meant to make you cry.*
I promise I will make you cry.
*But tonight I'm cleaning out my closet.*

What are you cleaning out, Marshall? Your cabinet?

I'm cleaning mine out, too—my cabinet of poisons.

I don't have much in it beyond my hatred and a few tidbits I've read. Arsenic, for instance, is deadly for an adult in a dose as small as a tenth of a gram. It has no smell or taste. The only thing missing from the book was whether or not you can buy it at the pharmacy. Or I could put yew seeds in your eggs. I think twenty would do the trick. A little while back a little kid was killed by a huge dose of regular old salt put into his pudding. I read about it in the paper. That could be something for you, Vadim—and the parents of that kid should get some, too.

But there are also so many lovely poisonous plants you can just pluck by the roadside. Lily of the valley, laburnum, meadow saffron. You can get cramps, hallucinations, respiratory failure, and even heart failure from meadow saffron.

I'm not sure you've earned such a pleasant death, Vadim. Probably not. Spoiled, canned fish would be more fitting. That way you'll have convulsions and suffocate and on your death certificate it will say the cause was botulism. You'll eat any old shit. I could put twenty cigarette stubs in your noodles, put a bunch of pepper on it, and you wouldn't know the difference.

You never smoked because you placed so much value on your health. There was even a time when you decided you wanted to lose some weight and you started counting calories—for about three days. It cracked my mother up—but she assured you that she didn't want to lose a single ounce of you.

You always thought women who smoked were vulgar. Which is exactly why I tried so hard to become a smoker; unfortunately it always made me feel ill.

I wouldn't want to kill you with sleeping pills. There's no way you should be allowed just to fall asleep.

Unless you ended up in the pond behind the oak trees—in broken glass park—where my mother took Anton in early spring to catch frog fry, which he put in our aquarium. We watched as they transformed into tadpoles and then were astonished as their number started to drastically shrink. There were fifty, then twenty, then ten, and finally a single cute frog hopped out onto the carpet and opened its mouth.

I don't believe that you stepped on it by accident.

When your lungs fill with water, I want it to be very unpleasant—and the frogs should croak. And you should lie there for a long time before anyone finds you. And then, when you finally rise to the surface, like all waterlogged bodies eventually do, you will look exactly as you deserve to, greenish-gray, rotting, bloated.

I would love to identify you then and say, "Yes, of course it's him—instantly recognizable, couldn't be anyone else." Others might not have seen it, but that's what you always looked like to me.

Dissolving him in hydrochloric acid would also be a nice trick.

But to keep such a big container of hydrochloric acid on the balcony and put Vadim in piece by piece—Maria would definitely think it was unhygienic. And in this case, she would actually be right. And you are straying into the realm of the ridiculous, Ms. Naimann.

What are we singing now, Marshall?

*And Hailie is big now, you should see her, she is beautiful.*
*But you'll never see her; she won't even be at your funeral.*

Exactly. But not Hailie. Alissa.

Felix was so pissed off I wouldn't come to Tenerife that he swore he wouldn't send any postcards. He told me on the phone, and I could hear tears of anger in his voice. And I could hear Volker in the background saying, "I'll send you one."

Felix slammed down the phone, but Volker called back.

"We would have been thrilled," he said. "But I can understand if you don't want to go. Or if you have something else to do."

"Maybe another time," I said to him. "Maybe next year. If you still want me to go."

"Next year I definitely won't want anyone to go," Volker said, sounding sad, not joking. "I already know I'm going to need a vacation after this vacation. Felix, I don't want to hear language like that in this house."

"My influence," I told him. "See, it's good that I'm staying home." Then I wished him a safe flight and good weather.

I run to the mailbox every morning. But there haven't been any postcards yet. There wouldn't be even if they had sent one—the mail takes ages.

I still jump up every time I hear the sound of the postman's bicycle through the open window.

I actually do have a job. But I only got it after I told Felix and Volker I couldn't go. I tutor three kids, all boys, in French. I get five euros extra for going to their houses. I don't feel like having them sit at my desk.

One of the boys, Kai-Julian, is even worse at his vocabulary words now than when I started. "I'm afraid," whispered his mother out in the hallway, "that he has a crush on you. He always wants to put on a clean outfit before you arrive."

She's one of those women who looks as if she was born with perfectly coiffed hair and makeup on. She's always at home when I go over. Sometimes she's smoking, sometimes she's writing out a shopping list, sometimes she's painting her toenails. Other times she is smelling the lilies in her garden.

During the hour-long tutoring session she comes in at least five times—to bring us tea, to offer us cookies, to remove the tea cups, to water the cactus on the windowsill, to tell me what the teacher told her about Kai-Julian. Sometimes she'll talk for fifteen minutes about Kai-Julian, and all the while he is sitting right there and his translucent ears are getting redder and redder. "He is poorly organized and is unable to concentrate," she says. "Have you noticed that, too?"

"No," I lie.

But I don't care as long as I get my money.

I also help Angela every day. For free. Just for the sake of it. I saw her crying in the staircase, pressed against the green wall right where it says "Sascha! Loves! Anna!" She has to take an exam in the fall or else she will have to repeat. She's already been left behind once—and she started school a year late. She was sobbing about how she couldn't stand the little shits in her class who were three years younger than her but who could already do everything better. And they looked down her shirt. How awful.

"If you want," I told her as she sat there with mascara smeared around her puffy red eyes, "I can help you prepare for the test."

She didn't understand at first.

"What do you mean—prepare?" she asked. We speak Russian to each other, but her Russian is almost as bad as her German. It's strange, the gibberish people around here speak in. Okay, so they can't learn the new language. But how do they manage to forget the old one?

"What do you mean—prepare?" I said, imitating her. "It's simple. I come to your apartment, you open a book, I explain things, you solve the problems, and you start to understand more and more. Ever tried that?"

She shook her head morosely. So morosely that it was as if I had asked whether she started her day with group sex.

"But," she asked, "why?"

"Maybe so you can pass your stupid exam?"

At this point she started crying again. I watched with fascination as the lumps of mascara stuck her eyelids together and she wiped them away with her hand and rubbed the black clumps between her fingers. Then she wiped her fingers off on the wall.

"I don't know," she said, which I found hilarious.

"We're doing it," I said. "A little bit of studying. It's not fatal. You won't get addicted. No chance of that."

"And what if I still don't pass the fucking exam?" she asked.

"Yeah?"

"You'll get angry."

I laughed. "You have no idea how angry I'll get," I said. "If you fail, you better steer clear of me."

Then she laughed, too.

I go to her place every morning around ten. I get up a half an hour before that and shower and eat breakfast, while reading a book. Maria and Anton have already gone to the pool and Alissa is off at kindergarten. It's the best part of the day.

Almost every second day I have to ring the bell for ages and kick the door just to wake Angela up. She always opens the door just as I've given up and am about to head back to our apartment. Then suddenly the door opens and she appears in her pajamas, with a teddy bear, her dyed blond hair sticking up, lines from the pillow pressed into her face.

"Huh?" she says. "Who is it?"

"Huh?" I say. "Integers?"

Then she snaps to. "Shit," she says, depressed. "Fucking shit. I was having such a nice dream."

She always takes off her pajamas as if I'm not there and puts on a miniskirt or something else along those lines. She has pale, milky-white skin and there are always bluish mother-of-pearl-like splotches on it. She changes in seconds flat and then makes a cup of instant lemon tea. Then she pulls out a slice of bread, toasts it, tops it with a piece of cheese, a thick slice of salami, and—struggling, her tongue out—squeezes a spiral of ketchup on top, and then sits down next to me with all the enthusiasm of a galley slave.

It's a shame nobody has ever videotaped us. Angela's not completely idiotic, just in spurts. Sometimes she understands things, though most of the time she's completely lost. She needs her fingers to help count. She often holds up her hands in front of her face as if to shield herself from a math problem she's just glimpsed.

"They're just numbers," I say. "They don't bite. You have to play with them."

"Play?" she asks, looking at me horrified. She's afraid of me, like Maria. I try to remain patient with her, but I've yelled at her a few times.

But that's not the only reason she cries. She's plagued by fundamental doubt. She cries at some point during almost every session.

"I don't understand anything," she often says. "Why do they want to torture me with this stuff?"

"So your pretty little head doesn't just float away because it's so light and empty," I say. "Or maybe you think you wouldn't even miss it?"

"What?"

"Nothing."

"I'm going to fail," Angela says. "I know it. Do you really think my head is pretty?"

"It's okay," I say. "But I'm not a boy."

Still, it's not as if our sessions are worthless. She is getting a little better. When she understands something, she flushes with happiness. She looks down and waits with rosy cheeks for my praise.

"See," I say, "you can do it if you just set your mind to it."

"It was just luck," she says. "I'm telling you, I can't do math."

"But you just got that right."

"Like I said, it was by accident."

"You don't have to be coy with me. I know how much trouble you have with this stuff. But you got that right."

She leans back over the books with a look on her face as if she's about to throw up.

It's strange that I never see Grigorij in the apartment.

"Where's your father hiding?" I ask one time. "Does he work mornings now? I haven't seen him in ages."

"He's in his room," says Angela.

"Why—is he sick?"

"He's drinking," Angela says casually. "He usually drinks all night long. Then he sleeps like a log all morning."

A chill runs through me.

"Is that something new?"

"What?"

"That he's so hardcore."

Angela shrugs her shoulders. "He used to do it once in a while," she says. "But it used to be rare. After three weeks he'd be clear-headed again and wouldn't drink at all for six months or so. It was no big deal. But it's been two months straight now with just a couple of days off."

"Holy shit," I say. "Why?"

"I don't know," Angela says. "Maybe because that fat-ass in your apartment threw him out."

"How does he make it to work?" I ask.

"How could he go to work—on all fours? He got fired."

"He was a . . . "

"Cab driver. Good job. Always worked nights. And I had peace and quiet here."

I look around, forgetting the math for a minute.

"Who takes care of the household here?" I ask. "I thought he cooked and ironed."

"Household?" Angela looks at me, bewildered.

"Yeah, I mean, everything's cleaned up."

"Only my room's clean. Nobody cleans the rest of the place. I don't have time. I have to study."

I laugh.

"What?" Angela says angrily. "It's enough that I do the shopping and cook. What else should I have to do? You have it good, that fat old lady does everything."

"Don't talk about her like that," I say automatically. "Anyway, she's not old. She's only thirty-seven."

"So? My father's thirty-six and he ain't young."

"What?" I blurt. "I thought he was at least fifty."

"Listen," says Angela, "are you here to talk about my father?"

I hunch over a piece of paper with an equation on it.

As I'm leaving I look around furtively. There are three other doors off the hallway. They are all closed. Behind one of them is Grigorij. I hold my breath but can't hear anything. I can't believe he's been lying here every morning and I didn't realize it. I thought he had avoided being around when I was there. Now I also notice that there are dust bunnies the size of tennis balls in the corners. And that the winter jackets are still hanging in the entryway.

"Where are all the empty bottles?" I ask.

"In the garbage," says Angela in an irritated tone. "What would possess you to ask that? Do you expect me to leave them sitting around? You sure are curious. It's not like your place was always dry."

"It was, actually," I say blankly. "Even Vadim. At least compared to everyone else around here. How long will your father keep doing this?" I ask. "When does it stop?"

Angela doesn't look at me. She looks at herself in the mirror. She's pretty plump—about twice as wide as me. She's wearing hot pants that cut into her light skin and a leopard-print bikini top.

I notice for the first time that she has a piercing in her belly button. Steel-colored with a blue stone in it. When she's sitting down there are folds on her stomach and you can't see her belly button.

It also occurs to me that it would look better on me.

"When he dies, I guess," says Angela, and turns away from the mirror.

"What do you mean?"

"You just asked when my father would stop. And I'm saying he'll stop when he drinks himself to death. Are you leaving now? I have to meet someone."

I walk out with my books under my arms. I find myself wondering why a feeling of shame is once again washing over me.

Then suddenly I'm all pissed off.

Maybe I've looked in the mailbox one too many times. There's still nothing for me in it. All of a sudden I can't take it anymore.

I never wanted to wait around for anything like that—a postcard, a text message, a call. I'm not one of those stupid girls. It's not the end of the world for me if some asshole doesn't stay in touch. Nobody to blame but himself. Or the post office. The mail can take weeks. And he's not going to write the first day of his vacation, the jerk.

Sascha doesn't wait around.

But she is waiting right now.

I'm starting to hate myself for it. As well as the person who hasn't written. I'm not sure which one I mean. Volker and Felix have merged into one single person who is enjoying himself on an island somewhere, looking out at the ocean, letting white sand trickle between his fingers, cracking open coconuts or whatever, and all the while not thinking about me at all.

I decide to stop running to the mailbox all the time. And not to get on the phone when they're back and call me. If they call. They can kiss my ass.

I ride my bike downtown to return some books to the

library. I check out a couple new ones and sit down outside on a warm stone wall. Behind me a briar of dark-pink dog roses are in bloom and it annoys me that they are thriving so prettily when I feel so miserable.

I don't notice at first when someone addresses me. I often don't get it when someone tries to chat me up.

"Did you leave your hearing aids at home?" says the person. I look up and can't help but smile.

What I see: blond, blue eyes, sunburn on the face and upper arms. Male.

I stop smiling and my eyes return to my book.

"Hello? I guess I'll have to talk a little bit louder."

I have to smile again.

All of a sudden he sits down beside me, so close that I shift away a little.

"Hot," he says.

"Uh-huh."

"The wall, I mean. Doesn't it burn your legs in those shorts?"

I look at my legs. So does he, intently.

I look back at my book.

"I keep asking myself whether we know each other," he says, his gaze still lowered.

I close the book.

"I've been asking myself the same thing," I say.

"So," he says cheerily, "have we met somewhere before?"

"I'm not sure if it was you," I say. "But one time when I was downtown on my bike, my chain came off. I squatted down to put it back on and suddenly there was someone standing next to me offering to help me. I thanked him without looking up, then I did look up—and you know what?"

"What?"

"Turns out he was—how should I put it?—he was an exhibitionist."

"Huh?" His jaw drops. "He . . . his pants . . . ?"

"Yep." I lift my face up toward the sun. It's fun to make somebody uncomfortable right off the bat. "To put it in the most genteel way, he exposed himself."

"And he looked like me?" he asks.

"No idea," I say. The best part is that it's all true—the bike chain, being downtown, everything. And all I can remember is the person had blond hair not entirely unlike this guy here. "I wasn't really looking at his face."

"What were you looking at?" he says flatly.

I shrug my shoulders. If I were in his place, I could think of a thousand funny retorts in the time he just sits there staring at me. But that's all he does—sit there thinking about my words. Or maybe about something completely different.

"Well, it wasn't me," he finally says.

"Too bad," I say. He looks at me blankly, not getting the joke.

How should he know what I'm thinking. How should he know that the fog I had managed to banish for a little while is back again, filling me from the tips of my toes to the ends of my hair. It's probably about to waft out of my mouth. I shut my lips tight.

I'll make a last desperate attempt to cast it off. I'll go out with anyone who talks to me right now, and do anything—the dirtier the better. If I piss myself off, it'll make me feel better.

That's what I'm thinking as I look the guy over. He's not unattractive. The best thing about him is his gleaming white T-shirt that's clearly just been ironed. I'd love to know whether it smells good like fresh laundry. He could almost be nice if he wasn't so slow on the uptake.

Still, nobody else has chatted me up, so I'll take what I can get.

"What did you want anyway?" I ask.

"What do you mean?"

"What did you want from me? Did you want to ask me something?"

"Huh? Oh, yeah. Ask something, right. Do you want to come to the city fair tonight?" He says it quickly, looking past me. It's not a very effective approach. I look right at him and he seems to get a bit uncomfortable as I hold his gaze.

"Why?" I ask. "Why did you want to ask that?"

"Just because," he says, glancing at me briefly and then looking away again.

City fair, right, of course, I think. Rollercoasters, cotton candy, haunted house. What else. A merry-go-round where they spray you with water. Upside down, spun around like in a washing machine. Betting who will puke first.

"How old are you?" I ask.

"Twenty-four."

"Really?"

"Yeah, why?"

"What do you do when you are not at the city fair?"

"I'm a college student."

"Engineering?"

"No, I dropped out of that. Computer science."

"Here at the technical college?"

"Yeah, why?"

"Where there are a hundred and thirteen boys and two girls?"

"Five girls. So?"

I don't answer. I think. He's not exactly a thrill a minute. But this fog isn't too much fun either.

I've got to get out of here. Maybe the city fair will be just the ticket.

"What's your name?" I ask.

"Volker. What? Why are you looking at me like that?"

"Really? Volker?" I ask, intrigued. It's as if someone has found a secret password in my mind and revealed it to him.

"Yeah, why?"

"No way. Hardly anybody your age is named that," I say, though now I'm having a hard time talking.

"Do you want to see my ID?"

"Yes," I say.

"What, right now?"

"Yes."

He reaches into his pants pocket and fishes around, unable to find it at first. Then he shows me his driver's license. That tips the scales.

"We can meet up tonight," I say. "But not at the fair. Let's meet in North Park. Do you rollerblade?"

"A little," he mumbles. He doesn't look thrilled. "I'm not very good."

"Perfect. Me, too. Eight o'clock at the main entrance? In rollerblades?"

"Okay," he says, doubt written all over his face. He's probably already regretting having chatted me up. Maybe he won't even show up.

But if he does—well, then I'll be out with a Volker tonight.

He does. From the first glance two things are clear. One, from the way he's holding on to the metal fence it's obvious he's very shaky on skates. Two, he doesn't appear to be exactly bursting with anticipation.

It changes a bit when I skate up to him and grab hold of him.

"Nice dress," he says, nearly losing his balance in the process of saying it.

I don't like dresses. I almost never wear them. But sometimes they're very practical, I think, though I don't say any of this, as he'd probably hop out of his rollerblades prematurely.

We take a spin around the park. He holds my hand as we do—not because it's romantic but because otherwise he'd fall. It's tough to skate that way, with our sweaty palms clamped together. And my arm gets stiff because I have to hold the guy upright.

We do all the things you're supposed to do on a first date—if you are in the fifth grade. We don't talk. We stop at an ice cream stand where, in line, he finally lets go of my hand and I shake out my arm. I don't bother to conceal my relief.

We eat our ice cream on a bench and crumble up the ends of the cones and toss them to the pigeons. Then I drag him deep into the park where couples are scattered around the grass. His hand is even stickier now from the ice cream. I would love so much to be able to wash my hands.

He stumbles at one point and pulls me down with him. Then once we've both gotten up again and lumbered over to each other, he kisses me. Out of the blue. I barely manage to spit out my gum. Afterwards he seems very happy, and I am happy, too, because he ate mint ice cream and the flavor makes me think of something far away and pretty.

I figure he's ready. So I pull him to a patch of lawn that's still free, behind a lilac hedge in full bloom. As I let myself fall to the grass, he stays upright, looking around as if he's lost his way in the dark woods.

"What's up? I say. "Are you worried about ticks? Or mites?"

"N-n-no," he answers. I hadn't realized he stuttered a little. Maybe he hadn't done it earlier.

It takes all my self-control not to laugh.

"Are you really twenty-four?" I ask.

"Just turned," he says.

"Can you help me get these heavy things off?" I ask.

"What things?"

"The rollerblades."

"I'll try," he says, wiping the sweat from his brow. "Man, it's hot here."

He kneels down and gives me another kiss. Then he starts working at the buckles of my inline skates. Finally he has my foot in his hand and asks, "What are you laughing at now?"

"It tickles," I say.

He lets go of my foot and lies down next to me. He plucks a blade of grass and starts to run it along my arm, from my fingertips, past my elbow, up to my shoulder, and on to my collarbone. I wonder whether he thought that up himself or saw it in a movie. It's all I can do to keep a straight face. It tickles.

Then he traces the same route with his pointer finger. Collarbone is once again the last stop.

He looks into my eyes. I look away so as not to laugh. Then I turn back to him and we make out in the soft grass for a little while—until he starts working at my arms again.

I'm dying to ask him whether all computer science students are so hesitant, but I contain myself.

I roll onto my stomach and bury my face in some daisies. I feel the blade of grass on the back of my knee. It heads down toward my feet, as if this guy has never heard of the practical aspects of a skirt. But then again where would he have heard about it, with only five girls in his department.

It dawns on me that the night isn't going to go according to plan unless I push him along a bit. Not that this is so awful, but I just don't have forever. Back home I've just started reading interviews with the American surgeon Robert White, who wanted to transplant heads. It worked on monkeys.

I turn onto my side, prop myself up on my elbow and look pensively at the guy in front of me. Short blond hair, pale face, light eyebrows. He's chewing on this sorry blade of grass and blinking his eyes nervously.

"What's the deal with you, Volker?" I ask.

How can it be so difficult to say a name? It's just a word. The most painful word in the world.

He frowns.

"You mean, how far along am I towards my degree?"

"That, too," I say. "Do you not find me attractive?"

"Of course I do," he says quickly. "Very. Lie back down."

I fall expectantly onto the grass and look up at the sky, and then feel his hand on my arm again. And once again he stops at my shoulder.

I really have to use every ounce of restraint not to flinch and giggle.

"You are so thin," he says quietly. "Incredible. I really like that. How do you do it?"

I forget to eat, I think to myself, annoyed. Not to please you, you wax-faced jerk. But because I usually have other things on my mind. I think of Clara, the anorexic girl in my class who comes home once in a while between stays at the clinic. And Katharina, who wears long sleeves in the heat of summer because she constantly cuts her arms with her father's razor. Not to try to kill herself, just to cut lines in her skin.

But in summer—or in gym class—the long sleeves stick out a lot more than a few slits would. There's something creepy about the long sleeves because they are clearly concealing something. Katharina seems to know this, too. Sometimes she looks proud of the reaction she gets.

I don't understand either one. Starving yourself or cutting yourself. I mean, it's idiotic to take out your anger on your own body. And pointless. It should be enough to be the target of everybody's ridicule.

I have to consider the fact that what I'm doing right now is not so very different.

But I don't want to quit halfway through. If I get up this minute and go home, it's possible that I might end up grabbing for a razor blade in the bathroom and testing that out. What a feeling. If Katharina does it so often, maybe it would do me some good.

It's getting cooler.

"Listen," I say, irritated, "is it possible you're shy?"

"Me?" He opens his mouth and forgets to close it again. "Why would you think I'm shy?"

"I don't want to lie around here in the grass all night, you know."

"Where would you rather be?"

I look at him for a long time. We just don't understand each other.

Suddenly he flushes, turning red beneath his sunburn, and begins to stutter again.

"It's j-j-just a little f-f-fast for me," he says. "I can't just do it straight away."

"You can't? How long do you need?"

"Oh, man. I've never met anyone like you before."

"You don't like me?"

"I do. A lot. You have an amazing body and nice skin, darker than mine."

"Yes, which is why I never get sunburned. Get that god damn blade of grass away from me. Please."

He tosses the blade of grass onto the lawn, thinks for second, then leans over and kisses me. I close my eyes so I don't have to see him. I try to imagine it is someone else. I guess Felix was right. All men are the same. If I keep my eyes closed, this guy isn't even here.

In that case the only person here is the one I picture. I put together an image of Volker's face from my various memories, building it like a mosaic from countless shards. But it slips away from me. I'm not sure anymore what he looks like. I can't picture his face anymore. And the more desperate I become trying to piece it together, the more details fade.

To distract myself, I try to figure out when the right moment is to alert this college kid to the condoms in my bag.

Just then my mouth is freed again.

"Have you overexerted yourself?" I ask. Immediately I'm upset with myself. I could have asked him that afterwards. If I scare him off too quickly, I'll feel really lonely and ugly.

"It's just weird that we don't know each other at all," says this other, false, blond Volker. He sounds tortured. "It's just not normal. Shouldn't we talk first?"

I'm taken aback. "We've already talked," I say. "But if you want to, we can talk some more. What do you like to talk about?"

"I'm sure you'd find it boring," he says sheepishly.

That's for sure, I think. But I say, "That's not true. What are you into?"

"Cars," he says quietly, in a tone suited to describing a first, shy, romantic experience of love.

"Cars," I repeat. "Cool. What kind of car do you want to have when you're all grown up and rich?"

"Porsche Carrera," he says without a second's hesitation.

There is nothing more boring than cars, I think, but answer competently, "I know somebody who wants a white Mercedes."

"Which model?"

"No idea."

"Mercedes are good, too," he says appreciatively. "A Mercedes would work. I'll never drive a foreign car."

I sit up. "Never? Not a Citroen, or a Volvo? A Saab? A Mazda?"

"All crap," he says, a look of disgust flashing across his face. "Never."

"Oh," I say, lying back down on the grass. The evening sky is gray with a few shimmering red clouds in it. The ground is getting a little moist. "You're a nationalist."

"Call it whatever you want," he says, twisting a strand of my hair around his pointer finger. "I hate foreign crap."

"Even Miele manufactures vacuum cleaners in Asia these days," I say.

"Miele? No way!"

"Yes, they do. Maybe not the entire vacuum cleaner, but components for it. Something. In China. I read it somewhere."

"Shit."

"I'm just saying, all that's left these days is foreign crap."

"Yeah, it's a shame," he says dejectedly. "We're drowning in it."

"Who—we?"

"We Germans, of course. Me and you. We're losing everything—our economy, our language, our genes."

"Our music," I add. "Culture in general."

"Exactly. In twenty years there won't be any 'we' anymore."

"It's horrible," I say. "Who will be left?"

"The Chinese and the Turks," he says, grabbing another strand of hair. He's lying quite close to me and speaking very softly. The crickets around us are louder.

"You don't like them, do you?" I ask empathetically, pushing my hair behind my ears before he can grab any more between his fingers. "The Chinese, the Turks, and other antisocial vermin."

"Fffff," he sneers. "When we take power, they'll get theirs."

"When we who?" I ask tiredly. I think I already know. "The Republicans? Who's funding your student group?"

"The Republicans? Ha!"

"Okay, so tell me."

"Guess."

"You're with the National Party."

"Hey, you're good." He probably thinks his kiss is sufficient reward. Now he's talkative and animated. He starts stuttering again. The talk is all about duplicitous politicians and fraud and *volk* and lost honor. I tune out.

I want to move on to something that has a little more to do with me.

"The Russians are worse than the Chinese, right?" I ask during a short pause. The sunset glows red in the sky above us.

"The Russians? Nah. They used to be bad. But you can forget about them nowadays. They drink themselves to death. They're degenerates."

"What can you do?" I say. "Bad food, bad weather, social injustice. The old dictatorship replaced by a new one. Arbitrariness and violence. How are you going to achieve world domination with all of that to deal with?"

"I'm not worried about them," he says. "It won't take long for them all to kill each other off. Anybody left will be in the slammer. And when we take power, we'll seal the border tight."

"Great idea," I say. "I'm all for it. Hey, you haven't taken anything, have you? You're clear-headed, right?"

"Of course," he says. "What do you mean—taken anything?"

"Some kind of mind altering substance. Anti-anxiety. Stimulant . . . "

"What are you talking about?" he asks, annoyed. "Drugs? I'm not crazy."

"What about rock and roll?"

"What?"

"Are you into it?"

"Huh?"

"I mean, we've already established you're not into sex and drugs."

He sits up. I remain lying down.

"You talk weird," he says.

"What do you mean—do I have an accent?"

"What? No, of course not. I mean what you are saying. It's weird. Do you vote for the Green Party or something?" He says this in a worried tone. He'd probably be less disturbed if I were a man in drag.

I don't want to bring to his attention the fact that I'm not even old enough to vote. And anyway, I'm not here for a political debate.

"So have we gotten to know each other enough?" I ask. I answer my own question as he rolls onto me and presses me into the cold grass. "Apparently we have."

The conversation has animated him. Now he's really passionate. I barely manage to move my head to the side—I don't feel like having to deal with slobbery kisses on top of it all. So he nuzzles my shoulder. It tickles incredibly.

The stupid thing is that I don't feel any better as a result. I close my eyes and then open them again. It's not very comfortable and it's boring. And the feeling of it doesn't really affect me. This isn't what I was trying for. I peer through my eyelashes and watch as he tosses the condom into the bushes, kneels, zips up his pants. I don't find it funny when he wraps his arms around me, presses his moist forehead to my temple, and whispers cheesy words to me—it was good, really good. I almost answer with "my pleasure."

I feel worse now than beforehand.

I put my rollerblades back on. It's nice to have them on again because my feet are freezing now. He groans as he struggles to put his back on. He can't close the straps. I help him in the dark.

"Want to skate a little more?" I ask.

"Where to?" he yawns. It's obvious he'd like nothing better than to crawl into bed—alone.

But I'm not done yet.

I skate ahead and he follows. Sometimes he cries out in the dark and I have to go back and pull him along by the hand.

As we skate around, I start to feel a bit better.

"Where are we heading?" he says warily. "I don't know my way around here."

"Who cares," I answer. "The path is good—nice, smooth asphalt."

"I guess so," he says tentatively. "I just hope we don't end up in the Russian ghetto. I think it's around here somewhere, isn't it?"

"Don't worry," I say, propping him up again.

We race through under the underpass, the wind whistling in my ears. I turn and look at him. I can't even manage to refer to him as Volker in my head. I watch as he smiles, spreads his arms out. His T-shirt flutters like a ghost.

"What a crazy night!" he calls out to me. "First you and now this."

"It's going to get even better," I promise him. "Look out for that stick."

His skates hit it and he falls. He rolls around as if he's seriously injured, but I'm not buying it.

"It got you good," I say, calming him down. I put out my hand to help him to his feet. "We need to cut through here anyway. The path gets bad up ahead."

"Through the woods?" he says, appalled. "Here? Are you crazy?"

"It's not really woods. Just through there is a clearing. There are big, beautiful oaks growing there."

He follows me. What else can he do. I know he'll never again follow a strange woman to an area he doesn't know.

"Being in the woods at night really awakes primal fears, eh?" I call over my shoulder. He grunts something in response.

There are fewer of them than I had expected. Five guys, two girls. They're sitting on the backs of the benches, next to a table that's been tipped upside down. In the middle of them is a hole in the ground, and in it a nice fire is burning. Peter is there with his two lieutenants, along with Anna and three others I've never seen before. But I can tell they belong—I recognize my countrymen immediately. Sometimes I can see it in the structure of their faces, sometimes in the clothing. And when nothing else sticks out, I can tell from the doomed look in their eyes.

I wave and then take off my rollerblades and walk barefoot. The skates are heavy and I hand them to Peter, who comes up to me and says, "Are you nuts? Barefoot? There's broken glass all over the place."

He doesn't look at me—he's looking over my shoulder at my companion, who is awkwardly following me, walking in his skates.

"This is Volker," I say to the group. In German. "He's a likeable member of the National Party, an activist for the party, in fact." They don't react. They don't know what the National Party is all about. "And these are . . . my friends," I say to my companion. Now the group starts to react, looking at each other with surprise.

"Volker's a little Nazi," I say, again in German. "I'm totally sympathetic."

He begins to quiver.

"What the hell is this?" says Peter in Russian.

"I don't know either," I say. "A whim. What do we have here, gentlemen?"

The upside-down table is covered with stuff. Spray cans, some of them in baggies. Plastic bags, half-empty bottles, jars, lighters, knives, cartons. It looks like a dirty little laboratory.

The next set of events takes place without any words. Peter points at me and raises his eyebrow. I nod. I feel at home.

I'm handed a rolling paper. Somebody sprinkles some brown crumbs onto it. Then on goes a clump from a bag of loose tobacco.

"Can't we make it without tobacco?" I ask. "My body just can't deal with nicotine."

"I have a water pipe," one of them says. "But it's at home. And I have no idea how it works."

"I guess this'll have to work," I sigh, rolling the paper up into a cigarette-sized tube. I've screwed it up and it falls apart. I was never any good at arts and crafts.

Peter takes it out of my hand, suppressing a smile. He opens it all up, rearranges it all, licks the edge of the paper, and rolls it into a perfect tube. He makes a show of twisting the end into a curly tail.

I nod appreciatively when he passes me his masterpiece with the words, "Ladies first." He flicks a lighter and the flame makes his hand jump out of the darkness. A warped version of my face is reflected in his ring, which is gigantic enough to pound nails with—or skulls.

I inhale with all my strength, sucking in as much as I can. My fear of the tobacco disappears. I'm not putting a lot of emphasis on my well-being tonight.

I don't cough, which is good. In fact, my body has no reaction. I sit there and wait and wait. Everyone stares at me. I stare back at them. Nothing happens.

"I don't feel anything," I say. "What the fuck. It doesn't do anything. Is that stuff any good?"

"I got that on a class trip to Amsterdam," says a guy sitting next to Peter. "We hid it in a piece of cheese. It's Moroccan black. It works. Wait, maybe it's Black Domina?"

"Rookie," says Peter contemptuously, grabbing the joint. It cracks me up, and Peter winks at me, inhales, and then exhales the smoke through his nose. He closes his eyes and passes it on. The next guy holds the joint like a flute and grimaces and makes faces as he inhales. And although I don't feel high, I find surprisingly warm feelings welling up inside me towards everyone here—everyone except one person.

"Like a peace pipe," says Peter, looking at me. He's acting as if there's nobody here but me. "Everyone gets a puff, right?" I nod.

The joint is handed to the phony Volker and he drops it.

Anna picks it up.

"I guess Nazis don't smoke Dutch grass," I say. "They just drink genuine German beer."

"We've got beer," says Peter. "Hang on."

He knocks over a can and amber liquid dribbles out.

In the distance frogs in the pond croak.

"Oh, sorry, I guess we're out," says Peter. "How clumsy of me. But who drinks that stuff anyway?"

Volker looks as if he's already tried everything here. He can't stop shaking and he's doubled over as if he's about to puke.

"It's okay," I say scornfully. "Nobody's going to do anything to you."

"You sure?" asks Peter in German. "I don't know. Want something to drink, you little fascist? Maybe a cup of sailor's tea?"

"Of what?" I ask.

"Haven't you read your classics?" asks Peter in a self-congratulatory tone, a proud host.

Volker shakes his head but Peter is already pouring clear liquid from a vodka bottle into a used paper cup. Then he adds a few drops of something from a brown medicinal bottle and stirs the concoction with a dirty knife.

"Legal speed," he answers in response to my questioning look. "From England. It's not something for you." He looks at the cup pensively, leans his head to the side, and then pours a little more vodka into the mixture.

I'm quiet like the rest. I don't say a thing as he approaches Volker and puts the cup into his hand. Volker's hand is shaking as if it's freezing cold. Peter wraps his giant hand around Volker's and says, "If you spill even a drop, I'll kill you. Do you have any idea what I have to pay for this stuff?"

He lifts the cup—his hand around Volker's—to Volker's lips. Volker closes his eyes. His head is shaking. With his other hand, Peter pushes Volker's head back. Then he pours the liquid in Volker's mouth, though the bulk of it sloshes down the sides of his face, causing Peter to issue a stream of comments, "I'll fuck your mother" the most friendly of them. I listen with my mouth agape. It sounds almost poetic. If only I could curse as fluidly as that.

Volker moans, grabs his throat, and falls to his hands and knees on the ground.

"Let's try that again," says Peter, grabbing the vodka bottle. I stay silent, as do the rest. Except Anna, who whispers in a panicked voice, "Honey!"

After the third cup, Volker groans loudly—it's almost a

scream. I look at him. He lies down on the ground, but sits up again, scratching at his throat.

When he starts to puke at my feet, I get up, grab my rollerblades, and leave.

Nobody stops me. Nobody says anything. I can hear the wailing and gagging from the woods. Then they turn on a portable stereo. The clearing is filled with frenetic beats that sound like a racing pulse.

I stick my feet back in the skates one more time. They hurt now. The fact that I didn't wear socks is taking a toll. The soles of my feet are raw and blistered. I skate anyway—through the neighborhood, past the Emerald, and out onto a main road.

I skate on the dividing line, right down the middle of the street.

I don't swerve to the side of the road when I hear a car behind me. The street lights are dull, I'm not wearing anything reflective, and my dress is dark—as are my thoughts. Just one thought, to be more precise. I'm pissed off that the Moroccan black hash has bypassed my receptors.

I guess I need something stronger, I think. I want to feel something. Right now.

And then it hits me.

I wonder how long this will last.

Brakes screech. I don't turn around. Everything's a bit slowed down.

A taxi careens past to my right and comes to rest on the sidewalk. I realize I am looking backward.

It also dawns on me that I'm falling and that now my knees are scraping along the pavement. For yards. Finally I feel something.

Not on my knees at first. It's my head wobbling back and forth as I'm wildly shaken and then rammed in the back. Suddenly I'm sitting on the sidewalk with my legs stretched out.

There's a small, swarthy man in front of me in a leather jacket. He's irate. He's cursing at me in a language I don't know, a language with lots of sibilant sounds.

I look over at the taxi, sitting sideways on the sidewalk, the driver's door ripped open, nobody at the wheel.

"Is that yours?" I ask. "Did you drag me through the street, you scumbag? You trying to skin me?"

He lashes out and a smack in the face goes pop in the night air.

"Little piece of sheet," he says.

"It's pronounced shit," I correct automatically, holding my hand up to my face. Then I look down at my legs. The skin is gashed open. There are streaks of red pulp from the knee to the foot. I forget all about this or that Volker, about the joint with no effects, about sailor's tea, and even Vadim.

I cry, quite loudly. Not because it hurts so bad—or at least not only because it hurts so bad. I cry because nobody is here to take care of me.

"Marina!" I shout. "You're never there when I need you!"

The taxi driver walks to the car. But instead of getting in, he starts rummaging through the trunk.

He comes back, leans over me, still cursing incomprehensibly under his breath, holding a bottle of the same brand of vodka Peter had. He unscrews the top and dumps the contents fizzing over my legs. My screams shatter the eerie silence on the street.

"Aaaah! Have you lost your mind?" I shout. "What the fuck are you doing?"

"Disinfection," he says, lifting me to my feet. "Otherwise infection."

But I can't keep my balance.

I sit back down and free my poor feet from the skates for the final time of the night.

"Where do you live?" the taxi driver asks acidly.

"Right around the corner," I say. "Thanks."

I put a skate under each arm and stagger barefoot to the

Emerald. The asphalt is warm. My legs feel as if someone is holding a red-hot iron to them. I'm standing in front of my apartment door when I finally hear a siren in the distance.

About time, I think.

I fall into bed without undressing. Thoughts race through my head. I'll never be able to fall asleep with my legs scraped open and these images in my head. I can't let the sheets touch the wounds. I can't lie on my stomach. I can't think about all that happened today. I don't want to toss and turn, but I can't lie still, either. I'm going to lose my mind.

Then I am swallowed by the great, merciful darkness of nothingness, and I don't dream at all.

When I wake up it's noon.

I have to think for a while about why I can't seem to move. Then I remember. I sit up and look at my legs. They are swollen in places and raw and red.

The skin will grow back, I think. There's nothing I can do.

I try to stand up. It works. I can walk, too, though it's difficult.

Sitting back down is harder. It feels as if the scabs will rip open again.

Oh man, I think, I can't stand around all day.

I make the mistake of leaving my room in just a long T-shirt. I run into Maria right in front of the door to my room. She's probably been waiting there. Maybe she wanted to ask me a question or tell me something.

But she forgets about it as soon as she sees me.

And I thought it wasn't that noticeable.

I brush aside her horror, her sympathy, her complaints, her iodine tincture, her entreaties to go immediately to the doctor, her praying that I never go skating again without kneepads—as if they would have done anything. The best one is her asking me not to go rollerblading ever again at all, and her wanting to keep Anton from ever doing it again, as well. She knew all along that something like this was going to happen.

"It's not so bad," I lie.

"How could you get so badly hurt?" she asks three times.

"I was drinking," I say curtly.

"You?"

I go into the bathroom and lock the door. From there I repeat that yes, yes, yes, it's already been disinfected. "Leave me alone," I say. It's not an order. I'm begging. Showering would be a bad idea, I think. I do have nerves, after all, and they'll relay the pain. I'm made of nothing but nerves. If only I didn't have any. That would be great.

Since I can only stand or lie down, I lie down in bed and read the Robert White interviews. Every half an hour, Maria brings tea with milk along with some pastries. The baked goods stick in my throat, but the tea I drink thirstily until I realize each cup is sweeter than the last.

"Are you putting an extra spoon of sugar in each time or what?" I ask gruffly. "Tell me. I won't yell at you."

"A half spoon more in each cup," Maria says, cowering in the doorway. She's afraid to come any closer. "It's all I can do for you." She tries to smile.

I don't know what to say.

The second day is worse. I have to take aspirin. The third day I'm feeling better again, much better. So good, in fact, that I hobble out to the kitchen and ask Maria how things are going.

She looks at me, startled, and says, "I don't know, why?"

I get pissed off by this highly intelligent answer.

Then I compliment her on the chicken in walnut sauce she's just made. You can eat it hot or cold. It's the best dish from the Caucuses.

"I wish I could cook," I lie, without any real inspiration.

"But I don't think I'll ever learn how. Marina couldn't really cook, either, and never really wanted to. I guess I inherited that from her. I mean, I guess I have other talents. Anyway, do you think you could teach me?"

Panic spreads across Maria's face. She looks back and forth between my face and the sage plant on the windowsill. She looks a bit like Angela as she does.

I can see the wheels turning feverishly in her head as she tries to figure out what kind of trap I'm setting and what consequences it will have for her.

"Me teach you something?" she stutters helplessly at the sage.

But I'm not listening anymore because a funny thought has occurred to me: if Maria became Angela's stepmother, people who didn't know their story would instantly think they saw the similarities between mother and daughter, and both of them would want to shoot themselves as a result.

I find this amusing and start to chuckle. Maria, meanwhile, is on the verge of tears.

I take pity on myself and get up and go out for a walk. I know that back behind the closed door, Maria will shake her head for a while and then talk to her kitchen herbs about me—do they have any idea what's going on with Sascha?

Sitting on the bench in front of the building's main entrance is Oleg, who lives with his mother on the second floor. Alissa is sitting on his lap. I don't like it.

I'm not sure how old Oleg is. But he's probably already celebrated a fortieth birthday. Ever since I've lived here, he's been there every day sitting for hours on that bench. And why not—his legs don't work. He was hit by a car as a kid. Not sure how I know that. It's just part of the general knowledge here. He has red hair and rusty brown eyes, but he looks completely different from Felix. It might have something to do with the fact that Felix's face isn't covered with patchy stubble of varying shades of red.

I go closer and notice a lot of his stubble's gone gray since the last time I looked at him this closely.

Oleg always has a chess board next to him. He used to keep stacks of newspapers there, too, open to the chess column. But all the columns have migrated from the print editions to the web. The Internet is probably also why Oleg isn't outside as often as he used to be. When he's alone on the bench, he moves the chess pieces around. And if somebody sits down with him, he talks about whatever books he's just read.

Well, actually he doesn't talk about the books. He reads from them. But not from the book. From memory. Once I sat there next to him with the book he was reciting from and checked his memory against the printed copy. He never got more than five words wrong per page.

When somebody is that good at something, I'm not jealous. I'm awed.

My first year here at the Emerald I spent a lot of time on the bench with Oleg. Not to hear him recite stories. I don't have the patience to be read aloud to. I prefer to read things at my own much faster pace.

Nope. I played chess. He was damn good. He probably still is. I don't know anyone who has ever beaten him. He instantly solves any scenario in the newspaper chess columns.

No wonder he can't get anyone to play him anymore. Back then I was the only one who didn't get discouraged by the constant losses. I kept trying. I would take pride in the fact that I forced him to make fourteen moves instead of ten to reach checkmate. And he always explained afterwards exactly what I had done wrong. Each and every thing.

That first year I dreamed at night about rooks and knights and black and white squares. After school I would toss my backpack on the stairs and arrange the pieces on the bench even before I'd had a snack or done my homework.

I didn't listen to Oleg when he talked. I just stared at the board, looking up in amazement when after a while I would notice a group of boys had gathered around us. They listened to Oleg. And their ears were always flushed red. He talked to them while he casually made moves on the board and once in a while made some comment about one of my moves—those comments were the only words that got through to me during the games. He made those comments a bit louder, and I would say, "What? Yeah, yeah," and then shut my ears off again.

And then came the day I realized he was describing in minute detail scenes from the porn films he rented from a nearby video store. Each week the shop would pick up the previous week's videos and deliver a new batch to his apartment. And I realized he had probably been doing that all along as I sat there next to him thinking about strategies and attacks.

I was ten years old and it took me a while to connect the words delivered in Oleg's gentle voice with the giggling of his pimply-faced audience. I forgot about the game and listened with my mouth open in shock to the images he described with such precision. Some of the words he used sounded as mysterious as the chess terminology had before I learned it. With me Oleg talked of gambits, skewers, and castling. The things he talked about with the boys didn't sound much different. That certain number combinations and things like French openings existed not only in my favorite game but apparently also in his porn films seemed like a huge and particularly cruel betrayal.

It took some effort to close my hanging jaw. Then I gathered up my things and pushed my way through the circle of panting boys without saying goodbye. And since that day I've hated not only Oleg but also the checkered board. That was our last game, and that was almost seven years ago.

He's still sitting there and now my little sister is frolicking on his lap. For the first time in ages I sit down next to him on the bench. He still has the same chess pieces. The dirty white queen was the same one I used to use, and there was already a piece of the black king's crown missing back then.

"Watch," says Alissa happily to me, grabbing Oleg's thick wrist. "He can't break my hand!"

"What?" I ask, looking with annoyance at Oleg. He doesn't look any less sheepish.

"I told him to try to crush my hand until it hurt, but he can't."

"What do you mean?"

"Do it," Alissa orders Oleg. "As hard as you can."

Oleg's giant fist closes around her hand and his face goes red with feigned effort. Alissa squeals with delight: "It doesn't hurt! It doesn't hurt!"

Oleg smiles at me as if to ask forgiveness and shifts Alissa off his lap.

I'm speechless. I've just realized I used to play the same game with him during my first year at the Emerald. Even then he had enormous arms, as if to compensate for the powerlessness of his legs. The idea of testing that strength excited me, too.

And I celebrated the same way when I withstood his grip without pain.

"Let him do it to you," says Alissa.

I remain gloomily silent.

"Long time," says Oleg. His voice is more gravelly than it used to be.

"What do you mean?" I say. "I see you every day."

"But not close up. What happened to your legs?"

I shrug my shoulders. I've never forgotten what he was talking about that time during our last game together. I can still see the images he was able to create in my head. And the stupid thing is that I didn't understand everything back then and ever since it's bugged me what he meant by this or that term.

"What are you doing with my sister?" I ask, gingerly feeling a scab on my shin as I do.

Oleg sits up straight and fidgets with his crutches.

"Nothing," he says, taken aback perhaps by my tone or by the look on my face. "What do you think I'm doing? I showed her a few chess moves. She's so bright. It's funny."

"Yes, she is," I say. "Who else are you playing against?"

"Nobody," he says, smiling his I'm-so-sorry smile again. "I have a chess computer game now. But other than that, the general interest around here has dropped off. My three favorite retirees are all dead. And there's no younger generation. I mean, there is one, but they would rather shoot at monsters or grope Lara Croft."

It suddenly occurs to me that Vadim used to sit and listen to Oleg, too, with a disgustingly sleazy look on his face. And I'm sure Oleg wasn't reciting the latest Nabokov biography to him. And afterwards Vadim would come home and put his arm around my mother. Of course.

An evil thought enters my mind: I'm not the slightest bit sorry about his broken spine.

But then I remember that my mother often used to sit with Oleg, too. She would laugh. He would recite her favorite passage to her—from Mikhail Bulgakov. In a white cape with blood-red lining, shuffling with a cavalryman's gait, the Procurator of Judea, Pontius Pilate, emerged on a covered colonnade between the two wings of Herod the Great's palace, with a terrible headache, o gods, ye gods, why do you punish me so?

This was after I had sworn off chess. Once I asked my mother angrily how she could talk to Oleg—didn't she know what his favorite hobby was?

"What is it?" she asked calmly. I looked at my feet and mumbled something. She understood somehow what I meant.

"Sweetie," she said, "he's handicapped."

"So?" I answered angrily. "Serves him right. You should have seen how worked up all those little wankers were from his stories."

"You should be more understanding. He's handicapped," repeated my mother. I found it maddening back then. But now, looking at his aged face, it occurs to me that he wore sunglasses to my mother's funeral. He kept them on in the dim funeral home. It was the only time I've ever seen him in sunglasses. Right now, for instance, the sun is beating down and he's not wearing any.

"Shall we?" I ask before I think about it too much and change my mind.

He looks at me and raises his eyebrows questioningly.

"What?" I ask. "I haven't played for six years. And you? How many grand masters have you beaten in that time?"

"Four," he says meekly. "Online."

I take the white queen and move her to E8.

"You've forgotten everything," Oleg says. "Turn the board around. D1. But there are missing pieces. I have a new set at home."

He touches the keys hanging from a chain around his neck and looks at me hopefully.

"Give them to me," I say. "I'll go get them. Where are they?"

"White box on the bookshelf," he says, putting the keys in my hand. "Can you also bring something to drink?"

"Anything else?" I ask.

He smiles.

"Beer?" I ask.

"Soda," he says. "Or iced tea. Whatever you can find."

"Is your mother home?"

"My mother?" he says, shocked. "She died last year."

"What? That's impossible." I sit back down next to him.

"I think the same thing sometimes," says Oleg. "That it's

impossible. But it's true. I'm not surprised you didn't hear about it. What did you say?"

"Welcome to the club."

"I thought I had misheard you."

I unlock his apartment and open the door. I almost pass out from the stench. The place is a dumpster. First, I go into a room where a messy bed is surrounded by stacks of papers, books, and newspapers, piles of cassettes, and dumbbells. I find the white box of chess pieces.

I find myself standing in front of three color photos thumbtacked to the wall. They are newspaper clippings. In one photo a little Japanese girl is sitting on her father's shoulders. Above her is a blossoming cherry tree. The caption reads, "The earliest cherry blossoms since 1953 in Tokyo's Ueno Park." The second photo is of two sumo wrestlers during a match. And the third shows a smiling, red-haired woman.

My mother.

Nothing surprises me anymore.

I can't manage to go into the kitchen, even with my sleeve covering my nose. Instead I stop off for two glasses and a bottle of apple juice from our apartment.

Oleg doesn't say anything about it. Neither do I.

"Should I play without my queen?" Oleg asks.

"Why?" I ask, annoyed. "No way."

"Then at least with two fewer pawns? Or with no pawns?"

"Cut it out. I want to lose on my own. Without any help from you. It's enough that I'm playing the white pieces. Alissa, give me that."

I opt for the Sicilian opening despite the fact that I always found it awkward. It's the only one I can remember off the top of my head. I try to concentrate. But I just end up staring at the board while Oleg chats away nonstop and barely pays attention to the game.

"I'm reading a cool book right now," he says. "It's set in

Moscow. Bombs are going off all over the place. Like what's happening there these days, just ramped up a bit. A young married woman with a daughter cheats on her husband with a guy who claims he's an alien. He wants to free her from her personal hell, take her back to his planet, where everything will be better."

"Aha," I say, annoyed that I can't come up with a strategy, that I'm following stupid rules for beginners, and that Oleg's chatter is getting in the way of the few thoughts I do have.

"And the best part is that right up to the end, you are wondering whether he is for real or whether it's just a fantasy. They both toy with each other the whole time and then, man, it's so sad."

"What's it called?" I ask because I don't want to be rude.

"The Evacuator," Oleg says, his voice full of emotion. "It's so great. I got it on the Internet. I get all my books online now. There are a couple of good sites. I download them and print them out. I just need to get them bound—my place is so messy. Are you nuts? What are you doing?"

Then I too see what a stupid move I've just made.

"It's because of all your blabbering," I say angrily. "I can't concentrate anymore the way I used to be able to."

"Take it back."

"No."

"I'm telling you, take it back. You can do better than that."

"Leave me alone. I'll play how I want to. And I'm not taking back any moves."

"You've played great up to now. But there's a much better move to be made there."

"Take the pawn in front of the king," Alissa says suddenly.

"I think I can do without your tips," I say bitterly. "It's a trap. He'll just take my knight. Can't you see that?"

I stare at the pieces on the board, still no good ideas occurring me. Then I realize Alissa is right, and that my knight would be protected by a bishop. And for the first time in my life, I take back a move. It goes against all the rules—and against every fiber of my being.

"Well done," says Oleg. "Pretend you're a bird. Take off and fly over the board. Don't just stare at a piece, see the whole game. Let your soul stretch out its wings . . . "

"Shut up. It's chess."

"Aha, bold, risky, you want to attack, but we strike back, eh? What do you think?"

I chew on my fingernails and find myself unable to see the whole game.

"Not that way, Sascha. Take it back."

"Not again. It's no fun that way. I want to play on my own."

"Accept the help. You're just a few details away from being a really good player. You're just too tense."

"What a dumb idea to want to play you. If I were your chess computer, I would have exploded long ago," I say, taking the move back. I spend another six minutes thinking while Oleg whistles an annoying melody. He's probably having an incredibly hard time resisting telling the alien love story word for word.

"See," he says in a praising tone, "sometimes you only get it right on the second try."

I'm flattered that he now stops whistling and takes a full minute to think about his next move.

Then I dither again, unsure of myself, sacrificing pieces, attacking, get praised, cursed, and taunted. Then he stops whistling and begins to sing, "I'm still, I'm still Jenny from the block."

I try to decide which pawn to advance to take his queen. I've never managed that against Oleg. I'm even dreaming grandly of a stalemate.

"Take the move back," Oleg says as I'm happily buzzing

about my chances. "That was moronic. Think about it. For a change."

"Kiss my ass."

"Think. Spread your wings. You are looking in the wrong direction. Leave your pawns alone. The main attraction is up in front."

"I can't see it, god damn it. This is all I can do."

"What's the aim of this game?" Oleg asks. Then he sings, "Don't cry for me, Argentina . . . "

"What?" I roll my eyes.

"The goal."

And then I suddenly see it and shove my rook forward and shout "check" so loud that a fat pigeon pecking at sunflower seed shells nearby takes off in a huff and flies a few circles high above us.

I watch it go. I wouldn't have thought it could fly.

Then I look back down at the board, wait for Oleg's move, shift my king, and put Oleg in checkmate.

He's as happy as if I had just healed him with a wonder cure.

"Don't be ridiculous," I say, though inside I don't totally agree, "I didn't win. Not on my own. It doesn't count."

"Of course you did," says Oleg, beaming. "I barely helped you at all. Great game."

"We won," Alissa is singing. She climbs back onto Oleg's lap. "We won. We did it, not anybody else."

"I'm off," I say, putting the pieces back into the white box, closing it up, and handing it to Oleg. I get up. It's difficult to admit to myself how proud I am. And how close I am to feeling that things are going to work out from here on.

But I still don't like seeing Alissa on Oleg's lap.

The bomb goes off the next day.

I have bad dreams all night, as if I sense it. In my dream I'm thirteen again and am having my first try of an odorless liquid down in a moldy basement. It's a time when I still have friends here in the Emerald, and one of my friends' parents used to make up and mix what they called cocktails.

After just two sips, my throat feels like it's numb. I push the cup away and grab my neck. It feels as if I'll never be able to swallow again, to breathe again, and I wake up gripped with fear but still able to wonder at the fact that this long-forgotten memory has somehow been exhumed deep within my brain. I hadn't thought about it for years. I've also learned in the meantime that cocktails aren't drunk in basements and that you don't automatically see orange clouds and a dozen red suns after you drink a normal cocktail.

But the feeling of the edge of that cup on my lips is so realistic that I almost throw up.

I lie on my back and breathe carefully in and out. It's no longer involuntary. I breathe until I fall asleep again. This time I'm haunted by Grigorij, who is crawling on all fours to a taxi. Then he gets in and starts driving it straight at me. But instead of running, I stand still and wait for the car to hit me. It doesn't hurt at all. I make a fist and flatten Grigorij's face through the windshield.

I punch and punch and wake up from the pain in my hand. My knuckles are skinned.

Is it possible to punch the wall in your sleep?

Why can't I dream about Volker, I think angrily. Or at least Felix?

After that I don't want to risk falling asleep again. I sit up in bed, lean against the wall, and freeze. When it starts to get light, I pull a sweater on over my pajamas, creep out of the apartment, and walk down to the mailbox.

It's much too early for the postman to have come, and once again there's nothing in the box. Of course. Only the paper, which I pull out.

I scan the front page. I don't notice anything of interest.

In the elevator I look over the headlines. I still don't see it. A boring news day, and it puts me at ease.

I love boring things. They're comfortable.

I lie down in bed with the paper. But instead of reading it, I fall right to sleep. I'm awoken by the phone. It makes me jump—it's already after nine.

I brace the phone between my ear and my shoulder and gather up the pages of the paper. They're scattered around the bed and floor.

"There's no point in canceling, Angela," I say. "I'm going to come anyway."

But it's Anna.

"Is it true?" she asks without so much as a hello.

"What?"

"That he's dead."

"Who?" I ask. I don't know why she's asking me—I left broken glass park before she did that night. "Are you crazy, asking me that?"

But it's not Anna who doesn't get it, it's me.

"Him," says Anna. "Vadim. I heard that. My mother said . . . "

The phone slips and falls to the floor. The back comes off and the battery flies out.

"No," I say. "It can't be true. I didn't . . . "

Then I see it in the paper. A little box at the top of the page. "Emerald murderer dead."

"No," I say to the paper. "Where did you hear that shit?"

Vadim E. is dead, the paper says. I don't suppose they care that my head is spinning, that I feel nauseated.

"It can't be," I say. "I didn't kill him yet. I still have that ahead of me. I have so many good ideas for how to do it. I'm definitely going to do it. Kill him and write a book about my mother. Before he manages to do it. He'll never beat me to it. NEVER!"

I pull out the local section and spread it on the floor, holding it open with my knees so the breeze doesn't rustle it.

It takes some time for me to find it. Here, too, it's just a small item.

"Vadim E. has hanged himself in his cell."

"He left a letter."

I just can't comprehend the words in this blurb.

"No," I say. "It must be a mistake. They would have informed us. Somebody would have told us. There's no way they would let us hear about it in the paper first. No way. They must have made it up."

What a stupid article. A canard. Why is it called that?

I'll ask Volker.

I pick up the phone, put the battery back in, and click the housing back together.

The phone starts ringing immediately. The ringtone sounds somehow hysterical, I think. I should change it.

"Naimann," I say calmly.

Someone is whimpering on the other end.

"What?" I say. "Who's there?" Suddenly I'm completely disoriented. It's Vadim, I think. Despite his love for AK-47s, he had a pretty high-pitched voice, the old eunuch. Or maybe it's Maria and she's just heard about Vadim's death at the pool. Even though it can't be true.

Or it's my mother. The voice sounds so familiar. It could be her. It sounds as if she's hurt herself.

She's not dead, just injured, I think. Crashed her bicycle or something. How can she be dead? I got it wrong. It was all a nightmare. A horribly long one. And the night isn't over yet.

I don't say anything. I wait.

"Sascha? Are you there?"

Yes," I say. "I've been here the whole time."

"Please come. Please come now. Please."

"Where?" I ask. I don't know what kind of instructions to

expect. Go around the Emerald; there will be a white winged horse—get on and hold on tight. Or go around the Emerald to the broken phone booth; don't worry that it's not connected—pick up the receiver. Or go to the front of the building; a black car with no license plate will stop . . .

I would do anything right now.

"What do you mean, where? You know where I live. Take the elevator."

It's Angela.

"I don't want to right now," I say. "Leave me alone. Everyone just leave me alone."

"Please, Sascha. Please, please, please."

"Grigorij?" I ask. "Is something wrong with him?"

"What? Yes!"

Since I imagine Angela would make a cup of instant lemon tea before calling an ambulance even in an emergency, I run up to her place without waiting for the elevator.

I burst through the open door. I'm in the hall again, and all the doors are closed except Angela's. There are sobs coming from her room.

"Where is he?" I ask, standing there helplessly. Angela is lying on her bed in Mickey Mouse pajamas, crying uncontrollably into her pillow.

"Where is Grigorij?" I ask.

"He's snoring," Angela says into her pillow. "I only said it so you'd come. Would you have come otherwise?"

"No. Not today."

"See."

She starts crying again. I can't believe how much water a crying person can produce. She's spraying all over the place. I step back so as not to get hit. Then I hand Angela a pocket pack of tissues. She gingerly takes it, lays it on the bed, and wipes her nose on her sleeve.

I sigh.

"You should be glad he left you," I say. "He's not worth crying over."

"Who?" Angela asks, surprised.

"Mohammed or whatever his name is."

"Murat," Angela says with a smile. Her face is red and puffy. Tears are running down her face. The smile makes her look kind of crazy.

"Okay, Murat, whatever."

"He didn't leave me," says Angela. "Just the opposite. Tell me—what should I do? I just don't know. I'm . . . " She turns away ashamed. As if she's just correctly solved a math problem.

"Yes? You're . . . ?"

"I'm . . . " She rolls her eyes and bites her lower lip.

" . . . Dumb as a box of rocks?" I ask.

"No. Well, I am that, too. But no. I'm pregnant."

"Oh," I say. "Since when?"

"That's all you can think to say?" Angela asks, looking at a new blue spot on her upper arm. It's a strange-looking one. It's actually four round marks next to each other.

It looks like the imprint of a set of fingers.

Angela spits on the end of her index finger and rubs off the mark.

Why are her eyes so bright, I wonder. Is it because of the tears?

"What am I supposed to say?" I ask, clueless.

"Something."

"Should I say congratulations?"

Suddenly Angela becomes very matter-of-fact. "No idea," she says, sitting up and frowning. "What do you think?"

"Me? Why me? Why should I have an opinion about it at all?"

"You know everything. Everything's easy for you to figure out. What would you do in my position?"

"Use condoms," I say quickly. "Before it happened."

Angela sticks out her lower lip.

"What do I do now?" she says pensively. "Do you think Murat would marry me?"

"If Murat is anything like Mohammed, he'll be cracking jokes about the blond slut he nailed. He'll marry an imported virgin. And you're lucky there. Didn't I already say that?"

"Yep," says Angela, and I wonder—not for the first time—how she can listen to all of this and not defend herself.

"When did you find out?" I ask. "You weren't pregnant yesterday."

"Today," she says.

"Where's the test? Let me have a look at it. Maybe you didn't read it correctly."

"I didn't do a test."

"How do you know then?"

"I threw up. I felt really ill."

"Doesn't that always happen when you drink a lot the night before?"

"Yes," Angela says with a smile. "But it was different today."

"How?"

"It was a different kind of sick. Somehow a nice sick. I just couldn't stop puking. And afterwards I still felt nauseated. And by the way, we do use condoms. Most of the time. Until three nights ago, actually. The condom dispenser was empty. So fucked up."

"Three days ago?" I say, incredulous.

"Yes."

"And you think you're pregnant from . . . "

"Obviously. The night before that there were still condoms in the dispenser."

"Oh, man," I say. "You belong in the zoo, Angela. You can't be pregnant yet."

"Why not?" she says, confused. "Of course I could be."

"But you wouldn't know it yet. Your supposed child would

still be a cell making its way down the fallopian tube. It wouldn't be implanted yet. There would be no way to tell. What did you eat yesterday?"

"I don't know," says Angela. "All kinds of stuff. Jam. Something in tomato sauce."

I get ready to go. I'm afraid to ask whether she's heard anything about Vadim.

I wish I had her problems, I think. Actually, no, I don't.

"How do you know that?" asks Angela suspiciously, watching as I move toward the door. "That it's not attached yet. That I can't be pregnant. Yet."

"If you're worried, you can take a morning after pill," I say. "You should try to take it today. So it doesn't imbed. Just in case Murat did slip one past the goalie."

"What do you mean, doesn't imbed?" she asks, shocked. "I don't want that."

"You don't want what?"

"I don't want it not to attach."

"You want a kid?" I ask, dumbfounded. "You?"

"Not a kid," she says. "A baby."

"Well, you might just get one," I say. "It takes them ages to refill that condom dispenser."

I slam the door behind me.

The door to our apartment is half open. I go in and see the newspaper on the floor. Next to it, the phone. I kneel down.

It's still there. Vadim E. is dead.

And it wasn't Sascha N. that killed him.

That's when I begin to scream.

I scream like on that night more than two years ago. So loud that the windows rattle. So loud that echoes bounce around the staircase. So loud that people wonder whether they should call the police because somebody's been killed here again.

But nobody's been killed. He's already dead. He did it himself. And nobody warned me that I might be too late.

I stagger out of the apartment. There are already a few people hovering around. They step aside and talk amongst themselves. I walk past them without looking at their faces. Faces don't interest me. They're all interested in just one thing—getting off on whatever's happening at our place. Then they can call friends and tell them, and then those friends call their friends.

And then there is another hoarse scream and the sound of something heavy falling over. I jump and look up—the sound is coming from above—and my first thought is, Was that me?

A tremor goes through the people gathered in the hall—it's a soft sound, like a breeze stirring a field of grain. All faces look up. It sounds as if something is falling down the stairs. Or someone.

I hold tight until I see Grigorij in front of me, very close and all contorted. He's falling toward me and automatically I take a step to the side so I don't get buried beneath him. The noise he makes when he hits the bottom of the stairs is dull but ugly.

The people all gather around him with a chorus of "oh"s and "ah"s. One of them puts ice on his face, another pours clear liquid into his mouth from a small bottle. Oddly, a third person unlaces his shoes. I go closer and see someone open his eyelids and look with consternation into his eyes. Two women debate what number to use for an ambulance, though the assembled group is against calling one—"He's probably got a BAC of 0.4 again!" They're all afraid of the drunk tank.

I want to say something but Vera from the fifth floor (a trained engineer who these days works as a fortune teller at the train station—she's small, with dark hair and a fake tan) steps authoritatively in my way.

"Get out of here," she says. "And leave him alone."

"What?" I say, confused. "You want me to do what?"

"You people have already done enough harm here," she

says. "Just get away from us, you. Keep walking, don't say a word, don't address us, leave our men in peace, leave our boys in peace . . . "

"Me? In peace?" I ask, but she won't be stopped.

"And if you really want to do a good deed . . . ," this part she delivers with an appallingly friendly smile plastered across her face, "a Christian deed, then gather up your entire clan and move—and go somewhere far away, got it? Then we'll finally be able to sleep in peace around here again."

"What?" I ask, looking at her little hand, with six fat rings on it, waving me past. It's this casual motion that causes something in me to start burning, racing, and knocking again. Apparently she notices that and steps back, lifting up her hand in warning.

"Uh-uh," she says, and they all look at me. As they do, Grigorij, unobserved, rolls onto his side, puts his hand under his head, and seems to go to sleep—though there are still wheezing and rattling noises coming from deep within him.

"Move along," Vera repeats from a safer distance. The sudden tandem crying of the two-year-old twins on seven, Heinrich and Franz, is the only thing that stops me from going over and strangling her with my own hands.

"Okay," I say. "I'm going."

I hit the gleaming asphalt. There's nobody else out here at the moment. In the beating sun. It burns right through the soles of your shoes.

But the heat doesn't affect me.

I'm cold.

To the left of the building entrance a low stone wall is being built around a garden. It's about a third of the way done. Next year tulips are supposed to bloom there in front of the building. That's what the super explained to Maria when she stood there wondering why a pile of rocks had been dumped on the sidewalk and why as a result Alissa had to swerve out into the street on her scooter to avoid them.

I pick up a rock. It's quite heavy. I weigh it in my hand. A rock like this on Vadim's head—that would have been great. His skull would have cracked like a raw egg.

Too late.

I wheel back and throw the rock. It doesn't reach the window. I'm no good at throwing things.

Gym is the only subject I get a B in.

I pick up a smaller one. This time it hits with a crash.

I pause, fascinated.

The window shatters into a thousand glittering shards. For a fraction of a second they all hang in the air, a giant, weightless piece of art. Then they all plummet to the asphalt and break into even smaller pieces.

I chuck another. This one I throw higher. The window on the second floor is up. I hit it, barely. This time it doesn't shatter as nicely. Just an ugly hole. I look for another rock. I'm meticulous about it—it has to be the right size.

I'm getting better. Another windowpane explodes and crashes to the ground.

It feels as if I'm tossing rocks for a long time before anyone arrives.

I throw two more before the first scream rings out. Then the front door of the building flies open and people come streaming out. I take aim at them with another rock and they surge back inside, jostling each other to get in. Then they slam the door shut.

I laugh.

Everyone is scared of Sascha!

My muscles are starting to ache. I've blackened a dozen of the Emerald's eyes. But it has hundreds.

I have a lot of work to do.

I see Valentin lean around the corner of the building. He's

sweating, his face is contorted and red, his hair is standing up. He runs toward me and I wheel back to throw one at him. He ducks and runs back around the corner.

I can't tell who the person is who comes from the other side. He hides as soon as I turn in his direction.

I start to sweat all of a sudden, buckets, my entire body. My T-shirt sticks to my back.

I throw three more rocks. A curtain of glass shards rains down. The flowerpots on the windowsills are still there. A white face appears in one of the windows and then disappears again.

I start to laugh again.

All of a sudden there's pain. I don't understand what's happening. I put a hand on my left shoulder. Blood seeps between my fingers. There's a rock at my feet. Someone has picked it up and thrown it back at me.

But it's my left shoulder. I'm in luck. I can still throw.

I pick up the rock and take aim at whoever it is lurking at the corner of the building. But the person slips behind the wall.

I throw the rock at the building instead and it flies through an open window. The upper pane remains intact.

I hit with my next four throws.

And then I see them. Maria, Anton, and Alissa walking in the shade toward the building with their cooler.

A rock whizzes past my head.

Alissa starts to run. She's coming straight for me. Her mouth is open but I can't hear anything.

"Get away," I shout. "It's dangerous. Someone is trying to hit me. Maria, get her out of here."

Maria starts walking toward us. Her entire body jiggles. She's going to break apart, I think to myself calmly. Anton is behind her. He's crying.

I hear sirens in the distance. Finally, I think. How long do they expect me to keep throwing? I'm getting tired.

Suddenly Alissa is right here, clinging to me.

I see the rock coming from the corner of the building. I rip Alissa's hands off me and shove her behind me. But she's not safe there, either. Another rock whizzes toward us, barely misses Alissa's bare legs, and thwacks into my calf.

I feel the pain shoot through me. I think this must be what it's like to get shot.

I never see the rock that hits me in the head.

The sheet over me is as white as new-fallen snow. There's a spiderweb in the corner. It quivers a little. Maybe because a spider is dangling from it. Or maybe because a light breeze is wafting in through the window.

I stare at the web for a long time. There's no alternative. If I move my eyes it feels as if my head will explode.

I groan aloud, but that hurts, too.

So I just sigh.

Then I realize my right hand is sweaty. Someone is holding it. I lower my eyes as far as I can, but I can't make out who it is. I move my eyes to the right. There's something colorful there. I move them to the left. On that side is an IV drip stand wired to my left arm.

"Who's there?" I ask quietly, so it doesn't boom in my head.

"Me," I hear.

It's Maria.

"Am I sick, Maria? Stop crying. I'm still alive. I can hear you crying. Where is Alissa?"

"In kindergarten," says Maria, sniffling. And then she adds, "She's doing fine, don't worry."

"And Anton?"

"He's okay."

"What's that mean?"

"He's in a new therapy program. He's a little mixed up."

I remember everything.

"Am I going to jail?" I ask. "I did a lot of damage."

"I don't know," says Maria. "I didn't understand what they said."

"Is there a cop in front of the door?"

"No."

"Good."

I close my eyes. But I still see a lot. A thousand colorful bugs dance on the inside of my eyelids.

"How long have I been lying here," I ask.

"Four days," says Maria.

"Four days? Weird. Was I unconscious?"

"No," says Maria blankly. "You were conscious almost the whole time. You talked. You laughed a lot. I thought I was going to die when I saw you lying there after you got hit. Your entire head covered in blood. I thought you were dead. My poor little girl. So thin. All bloody. Your hair all messed up."

I feel something moist on my hand. Just for a second.

"What was that?" I ask. "Stop sobbing."

With great effort, I lift my arm and look at the back of my hand. There's a red mark on it.

"New lipstick?" I ask.

Maria doesn't answer.

"Did I laugh when I was hit?" I ask.

"No, you were out cold. You came to in the ambulance."

"Why can't I remember that?"

"Who am I? Moses?" asks Maria.

I laugh. She learned that phrase from Anton. Laughing hurts like hell.

"What's wrong with me?" I ask. "Do I have a concussion or a skull fracture?"

Maria sighs. "Yes," she says. "Fractured skull."

I try to move my arm again.

"Don't touch the bandages," says Maria fearfully. "You'll mess it up."

"Were the little ones here?" I ask.

"Alissa," says Maria. "Anton's scared. Alissa wanted to write something on your bandages. She said that's what people do. Said it would look better. I scolded her, but you said it was okay. Do you remember?"

"No," I say. "She should go ahead. Maybe she can draw a flower. Or a seagull."

"A postcard came for you," Maria says. "This morning. A pretty one. Do you want to see it?"

"Nah. My eyes hurt. What's on it?"

"On the front is the ocean. On the back is some writing."

"Do you have it in your hand?"

"Yes."

"Read it to me."

"I can't."

"Why not?"

"Can't."

"But why?"

"I can't."

"You're getting on my nerves. Why can't you?"

"Um, you know why . . . it's not in Russian."

"Maria!"

"And illegible. The only thing I can make out is at the bottom. Three letters. ILU. What's that mean?"

"You don't know?"

"No. How would I?"

"Well, I'm not going to tell you," I say.

"You shouldn't have come," I say as he walks into the room, unfazed by what I'm saying.

I turn away. I don't want to see him. And I definitely don't want him to see me. But there's nothing I can do now.

He takes three big steps and is right next to me. I'd like to crawl under the white covers and pull them over my head.

But I remain sitting up.

Sascha doesn't hide from anyone.

Then he puts his hand on my arm, bends down, and kisses me gingerly on the cheek. Very gingerly.

"I'm not made of glass," I say harshly. His hand wanders up to the base of my neck and stays there, warm, weighty.

"The other one, too," I say. He puts his other hand on my shoulder and there's nothing left for me to do but sigh and close my eyes.

"Hello, Sascha," he says.

"Hello, Volker," I say. "How was vacation?"

"Shitty," he says, but I can hear the smile in his voice. "But getting home was worse. Felix called you. He talked to your relative, your aunt or whatever. Or rather, he tried to talk to her. But he didn't understand. He came running to me screaming that you'd been stoned to death. Sascha . . . rock . . . head . . . hospital!"

"Her vocabulary has absolutely exploded if she was able to say all that," I say.

"So then I called. My knees were shaking. A chirpy little girl got on the phone and said that someone had broken your head—that's the way she put it—but that it would grow back together, your head. She said you could curse again already and that it sucked that you had been gone for such a long time."

I try not to laugh, and put my hands on his. They are much bigger than mine.

"And I asked her whether it was possible to visit Sascha. She said Sascha didn't want to see anyone but her. Said you didn't even want to see Maria, but that Maria went anyway—'she had to take me there.' I told her to ask whether you wanted to see Volker or Felix."

"She asked," I say.

"Of course, and then she told me that Sascha didn't want to

see those two people. She didn't want to see anyone, and if she didn't want to, that meant she didn't want to."

My laugh is a little too loud.

"I talk to her on the phone a lot . . . ," Volker continues.

"Huh? She didn't tell me that!"

"Because I asked her not to. Good to know she's so trustworthy. Yesterday she said the bones in your head weren't broken, or not really, and that the bandages were off and that tomorrow you would be coming home and, oh, did I have a car? I said yes. So she said, 'Why don't you bring Sascha home—she's not supposed to walk too much.'"

"Alissa hasn't gotten smacked often enough," I say. "Oh, I'm sorry, your shirt's a little wet now, here on the sleeve."

"Blind rain?"

I don't answer.

"Of course I told her I would bring her Sascha home to her. Then she said, 'That's good,' and just hung up."

His watch ticks loudly in my ear. I count along to it: thirty, sixty, ninety.

"I'm scared I'll hurt you," he says.

"What do you mean?"

"I mean this spot here. And over here. Does this hurt?"

"No. Not anymore. Everything feels pretty good now."

"Crazy. What was this about no broken bones?"

"Turns out it was just contusions and cuts. They couldn't tell from the initial X-ray. But there was no fracture."

"It looks terrible."

"Then leave, Volker. I already said you weren't supposed to be here."

"No, I didn't mean it like that. It doesn't look bad at all. It's just . . . it hurts me to look at it."

"Get out."

"No."

"I don't want you to see me this way."

"Yeah, I got that. But it doesn't look bad at all. Have you seen yourself in the mirror yet?"

"No. They only took the bandages off yesterday."

"Go over there to the mirror and have a look."

"No."

Volker sighs.

"You're even more of a pain than Felix," he says.

"Thanks for the postcard, by the way," I say.

"Thank Felix."

"Tell him for me."

"You can tell him yourself. He's out in the hallway. He didn't have the heart to come in. He was worried you'd be all deformed. Why he still wanted to come here at all is a mystery to me."

I shake Volker's hands off my shoulder, jump out of bed, and throw open the door.

The hall is long and bright. Plates rattle in the distance. They're about to serve lunch. It smells pretty disgusting. Always smells like cauliflower no matter what they're serving.

Felix is crouched against the wall opposite me. He jumps, startled, then looks up at me.

"You sure got a tan," I say as he stands up and begins to smile. The smile continues to spread across his face until he's beaming.

"I thought you were going to look terrible," he says, approaching me and stretching out his arm to take my hand.

"Be careful," I say, cringing a little. "Probably better if you don't touch me. Everything still hurts."

He drops my hand abruptly, as if it's just stung him.

"Are you happy to be going home?" asks Volker, who has come out with my backpack over his shoulder. I go back in and look under the pillows to make sure I haven't left a book or something. Then I kneel to peer under the bed for the same reason.

"No," I say. "I hate my home."

Felix looks away, looking frightened and hurt.

"Why?" he asks.

"Because it always reminds me of things I'd rather forget," I say.

"This is where you live?" Felix says when we reach the group of housing blocks.

"In the tallest one," I say.

Volker parks directly in front of the door of the Emerald and grabs my bag.

"They've finished the garden wall," I say.

"You weren't gone that long," says Volker. Felix is silent.

"Seems like an eternity," I say. "A few weeks in the hospital is time enough to start a new life. The windows have all been fixed. Did you hear what happened?"

"I read about it in an old issue of the paper when we got back," Volker says. "I don't want to piss you off, but I have to say it brought to mind that guy who tilted at windmills . . . "

"Who?" asks Felix.

The benches in front of the building are empty.

"Where's Oleg?" I ask.

"Who?"

"A guy. He's handicapped. He always sits here. I wonder where he is?"

Volker is silent now, and Felix pipes up unexpectedly.

"How the hell should I know?" he asks. "Is it really that important?"

"The thing is," I say, "around here you always assume the worst."

"Doesn't stink as bad as usual," I say in the elevator. "Or maybe it just doesn't stink as bad as hospital food. I'm desensitized."

"It's awful here," says Felix. I catch the look he gets from Volker.

"So?" says Felix in response. "It really is hellish here. What do you want me to say—that it's nice?"

"Only if you want to piss me off," I say. It comes out sounding oddly upbeat.

"People think these stains are still from my mother's blood," I say in front of our door. "But it's not true. It's just dirt. She was never out here. She bled to death in the apartment."

Felix makes a gurgling noise in his throat, repulsed.

"Hi, Maria," I say. "Please don't hug me. I'm still very weak. This is Volker. And this is Felix. This is Maria."

Maria is all shy as she shakes their hands.

"We spoke on the phone," she says in German, and my jaw drops. "Alissa, you mustn't jump on Sascha"—she's switched to Russian—"she's still very sick."

"Yucky," says Alissa as I kneel down so she can look at my head. "It's closed up! And it's not red anymore! When did they wash away the blood?"

"Right away," I say. "What did you think?"

"Do you have new blood now?"

"Yep," I say, "about five quarts. That's like five cartons of milk. Anton, come here. Don't be scared. Have a look—my head doesn't look that bad."

"Yes it does," says Anton, bracing himself in the doorway of the children's room. "It looks bad."

"My little brother, Anton," I say to Felix and Volker. "He's a bit shy."

"Tokio Hotel," Volker says, reading the band name on Anton's T-shirt. "I love Tokio Hotel."

Felix turns away with a look of pained embarrassment.

"Tea," says Maria, again in German. "And blueberry torte."

"Later, Maria," I say. "Later, blueberry cake."

"Later it won't still be warm," she says elegantly, "but rather cold."

"What, in this heat?" I say. "This is my room, by the way."

"Is that your computer?" asks Felix. "What is that—an external modem?"

"I don't want to hear anything about my computer," I say.

"I didn't say anything," says Felix.

"What kind do you have?" asks Anton quietly.

"A much cooler one," Felix says. "Anyway, something. I'll show you sometime. Who's that?"

"That's my mother," I say. "And that is Harry. He died together with her. That's the last picture ever taken of them. I took it on the balcony with Harry's new digital camera. You see, Felix, it's dangerous running around with Russian women. Life-threatening, in fact."

"But you've never been married," says Felix.

"How do you know?" I ask. "What do you know about me? Do you have any idea how awful I am? Let's get out of this room—it's too cramped. This is the living room. These are my mother's books."

"Who hung up all these Chagall prints?" Volker asks.

"She did," I say. "They're all hers. She loved his stuff."

"They're weird-looking," says Felix. "I don't want to say they're ugly, but they are weird. Why are the people flying around like that?"

"They're dreaming," says Alissa from below his elbow.

"Aha," says Felix. "We brought a little present for you. Volker, where is it? The one for the little kid."

"I'm not little," says Alissa. "I'm almost four."

"What is that?" I say, standing stiffly and squinting.

"I believe they are called flowers," says Felix. "In a vase. It really does take a while to recover from a blow to the head, eh?"

"Felix!" says Volker. He sounds genuinely angry.

"No," I say. "Not that. Next to it."

This time the gurgling noise comes from Maria's throat. Volker looks at her, worried.

"What is that?" I repeat. I go over to the table. Next to the vase with the three sunflowers in it are some strange objects—something in a plastic bag that looks like a shaving kit and that brings uneasy thoughts creeping into my head, a notebook, pens, a leather briefcase.

"Sascha," says Maria meekly, "not now, Sascha . . . I . . . forgot to put it away . . . I'm an idiot . . . "

I shove Maria aside and reach for the notebook. Loose sheets fall out, dozens of them, all covered with sloppy, erratic writing. The pages slip through my fingers, giving off a strange odor that makes me nauseated.

Felix gathers the sheets off the floor, looks at them, annoyed, and hands them on to Volker.

I reach my hand out and open the leather briefcase.

Newspaper clippings fall out—all of which I recognize—along with documents I've never seen before: a Russian birth certificate, an old union handbook, a gun certificate, notarized translations. I toss it all carelessly on the floor. I know whose scent is on it all.

At the bottom are photos. Four photos.

A big print. A red-headed woman in a tunic-like outfit, arms outstretched, eyes closed. On stage, in the spotlight.

I turn the photo over and read the description written on the back in large uneven letters: *My wife Marina in her theater.*

Another big one. A young blond boy with a school satchel. His eyes look nervous and he seems to be trying to hide behind the satchel.

On the back: *My son Anton's first day of school.*

A smaller photo. A smiling baby in a high chair, both of the baby's hands buried in the food on a plate.

The back: *My daughter Alissa tries solid food.*

An even smaller photo. A dark-haired girl on a bench with her feet pulled up onto the bench. Behind her the Emerald. On her knees an open book.

It looks very familiar to me, but I can't seem to place it. I don't understand what this photo is doing here.

Behind me everyone is silent.

No, not entirely.

Maria's breathing is labored. Someone shuffles their feet. Another one coughs.

"Bless you," says Alissa loudly.

I turn over the last photo and need a long time to read what it says.

Despite the fact that there's just one word: *Sascha.*

I put the photos back in the briefcase, stack the newspaper clippings neatly on top of them, and close the case.

"Maria," I say. "Blueberry tore. Now."

Nobody notices when I get up and quietly walk to my room and close the door behind me.

I straddle my chair and pick up the framed photo from my desk. If I close my eyes most of the way and gently move my head, it looks as if the faces in the photo are moving. Blinking your eyes really fast creates the same effect.

Hello, you, and you, too, Harry, I say. We haven't talked in a while. I hope you're not mad I didn't take you with me to the hospital. I was all alone there. I hardly thought of you. Only once, and I was glad you couldn't see me. Or could you?

And I also thought about how good it is that you two will have each other. Always. I'll probably always be alone.

I don't believe in heaven or hell. But I know we'll see each other again. There have been a few moments in the last few months when I thought that time was imminent.

By the way, are you guys aware of the fact that Vadim is on his way? I hope he leaves you alone. Maybe someone there can show him how to behave properly. Either that or perhaps there he'll be so small and you so big that the only trouble will be avoiding stepping on him.

What a cowardly, rotten thing to do—just to take the shortest, easiest route to you. Don't you agree?

The problem is that I can't get upset about it anymore. I've lost my fire. I'm sorry, but I'm sure you'll understand. It's just the way it is.

Our apartment is full of people right now who are eating, talking, and laughing. There are two new ones among them. I never wanted them to come here, but they've come anyway. And it seems like they are enjoying it. I suspect this won't be the last time they're here.

Of course I'm not crying. I just have something in my eye.

Anton is showing Felix his Gameboy, and they seem to get along well. Felix can't hide the fact that he loves being idolized. And Anton is walking on clouds because an older boy is paying attention to him.

Alissa is showing Volker how to write his name in Cyrillic. He's impressed by how smart she is. She's also really cute—and cheeky. And he's probably one of those guys who always wanted a daughter but never had one. It's really idyllic and everything smells like cinnamon. Maria also put vanilla sugar in the whipped cream, so the scent of vanilla is everywhere, too.

There's nothing left for me to do here. I feel as if they will all be all right now even without me.

You once told me that on your second day of first grade, you just got up and left because it wasn't interesting enough for you. And that during school holidays and later between college semesters you would always go away somewhere. Take a train or hitchhike, just because you wanted to see the ocean or the mountains. And how you took a job selling magazine subscriptions because they sent you all over the place, to Siberia, to the far east. There was nothing you liked more than hitting the road.

I don't care about seeing the ocean or the mountains. I want to go someplace where there are lots of people and where nobody will notice the way I look at the moment.

Your favorite city was Paris, a romantic holdover from Soviet days—"See Paris and die," they used to say. We were there twice together. It was nice, but I don't want to go there now. Its romance doesn't suit me at the moment.

And when we were in Rome once, I was overwhelmed by the heat and the dust and the rattling of all the mopeds. My nerves are too frayed for that right now.

Berlin is cool, but I want to go someplace where I don't understand everything around me for a change.

Which is why, Marina, I'm going to see how fast I can get to Prague. It was your favorite city, too—you had nothing but favorite cities. All I can remember about Prague is having my first ever Irish coffee. You let me order it in a café. And I remember watching a painter on a bridge. You don't get much out of traveling as a kid—all you remember are the pigeons and the ice cream and the time you got lost in a crowd.

I haven't done much with my summer vacation so far. You wouldn't be very impressed.

I put the framed photo back on my desk. It falls over. I stand it up again.

The backpack I had at the hospital is on the floor, not yet unpacked. I open it and rummage through its contents. Then I zip it up again.

I open the top drawer of my desk and take out the power cord for my mobile phone, a grubby baggie of marijuana—I can't even remember where I got it anymore—two old rings that belonged to my mother, both of which are too big for all my fingers except my thumbs, along with my MP3 player, my passport, a couple of scrunchies, a half-empty jar of aspirin, and a stack of money. I've been throwing all my money in that drawer. I just never thought of anything I wanted to do with it.

I stuff the money and the MP3 player into my pants pocket. The rest of the stuff goes into the backpack. Except the scrunchies, which I throw back into the drawer. I don't need them anymore. They cut off most of my hair in the ambulance and the rest of it when they changed my bandages at the hospital.

I look at myself in the mirror for quite a long time. Then I look for my old black baseball cap. There was a time when I was obsessed with it, but I think I may have given it to Anton in the meantime. Nope, here it is, under the bureau. I put it on and feel ready to venture out among people again.

After having a look at my fingernails, I cut them with a pair of paper scissors.

I fidget with a pen, unsure about whether to leave a note, and what to write in it. I put the pen back down.

It would be an exaggeration to say I'm in a good mood. But something is singing inside me—and the words aren't Eminem's.

In the foyer I stumble over my rollerblades—and then over Anton's. I can't imagine ever putting those things on again. I put on my sneakers and listen to the voices wafting in from the living room as I tie the laces.

I'm a little worried someone is going to ask where I am.

But it doesn't happen.

I step out and pull the door quietly closed behind me.

It's extremely quiet all through the Emerald. The only sound is a baby crying somewhere.

The bench in front of the building is still empty.

I throw my backpack over my shoulder, turn my baseball cap backwards, and head out into the sun.

## About the Author

Born in Yekaterinburg, Russia, in 1978, the author now lives in Frankfurt, Germany. *Broken Glass Park*, nominated for the prestigious Bachmann Prize, is her first novel. Alina Bronsky is a pseudonym.